THE HUNT OUT OF THE THICKET

THE HUNT OUT OF THE THICKET

Stories by John Morel Adler

WITH ILLUSTRATIONS BY LAURA JONES

ALGONQUIN BOOKS OF CHAPEL HILL 1990

Published by

Algonquin Books of Chapel Hill

Post Office Box 2225

Chapel Hill, North Carolina 27515-2225

a division of

Workman Publishing Company, Inc.

708 Broadway

New York, New York 10003

Design by Molly Renda.
"February Quail—A Sketch" was previously published
in 1978 by *Cellar Door*.

LIBRARY OF CONGRESS CATALOGING-IN-PUBLICATION DATA

Adler, John Morel, 1956–

   The hunt out of the thicket: stories / by John Morel Adler.

     p.   cm.

   ISBN 0-945575-06-8

   1. Outdoor life—South Carolina—Fiction.

2. Outdoor life—Georgia—Fiction. 3. South

Carolina—Fiction. 4. Georgia—Fiction. I. Title.

PS3551.D595H8   1990

813'.54—dc20   90-190

               CIP

10 9 8 7 6 5 4 3 2 1
First printing

In memory of Leopold Adler III

.   .   .   .   .

Special thanks to Max Steele and Louis Rubin, Jr.

CONTENTS

THE HUNT OUT OF THE THICKET

THE HUNT OUT OF

THE THICKET

Seventeen days after the letter, he has found the buck. He has lived on the farm for twenty-one years, hunted it for eight, but never seen sign like this. It is needed, too, because of the letter. He really doesn't know

which will make him stay in the woods all day: the deer, or those carefully etched words. In his mind they linger, causing him to stand still and eye the brittle soybean stubble as if it were a stage set: "but you depend on me too much and I simply can't be bound. You are too intense."

It doesn't matter, though, he says to himself, finding his careful gait, mashing his teeth. He hunts, walking slowly on the sides of his feet, keeping his upper body from jostling, the rifle slung on his shoulder steadied at the stock with his right hand.

Reaching the fringe of the field, he brings the gun into both hands, looks at the plantation of pines ahead of him, and walks through them to the swamp and the thicket.

.   .   .   .   .

It was there, in that silent fortress, that he found the buck. Just the day before, he came to it the same way he walks now: over the sandy hill of pines to where the swamp bottomed, and on the other side of a harrowed firebreak the bulb-based trees rose with a wet, cold air thick around their trunks.

Along that firelane he found its first sign: the rut, laid in the beast's instinctive roamings as it left its trail for the does in the colds of October. Limbing saplings chest high, raking and scouring the bark with polished antlers, it had vented its passion. Then hastily, under clusters of low-lying myrtles, it had pawed the ground clean and squatted, urinating down its hind legs and at the same time hooking its antlers in the overhang, snatching the branches in its mouth and rubbing them over its aromatic tear ducts, finally popping them off to dangle and point to the claimed turf with the scent steaming off the cool earth and into the nostrils of the trailing does. And in the pawings, around those violent rubs were the prints spreading the loam, punched deep. From it all, he knew the animal, a picture moving high into his consciousness like a grandly fluid collage—the wide and stable rack, broad chest and bulging neck, streamlined in the flanks with the layers of muscle and bone and sinew connected so that it could cut a right angle turn at a full run within a body's length.

He marveled at the sign for quite a while. Then he stooped and pinched up a handful of the soil in the pawing and smelt it. Vague, with the grit of the dirt, the strong smell of decay, there was the almost fetid odor, the musk. It made him feel somehow powered and incredibly alive; the air around him seemed wet and pure.

From that edge he then found the animal's path, and followed it into the swamp. The lone furrowed strand of matted grasses wound back into the bottom where a knoll rose and the thicket of small pines, rimmed by several myrtles and low brambles, was blocked out, green, amongst the deciduous growth.

Like an alien he paused before entering. All sound, even the wailing of a chain saw two miles distant, was blanketed by the chill of the air. With his first step, a twig snapped under his boot, and the animal left. Without consternation, not even fast or flushed, it blew once (a nasal utterance welling in the bottom of the lungs, passing through its nose and mouth like a quickly mashed bellows) and was in flight, bounding deliberately out the other side, its hooves through the dirt on the edge of sound, like axe-strokes in clay.

He didn't know how long he stood, staring. The excitement in his chest made his legs quiver. For some reason, there in the cold, he considered turning and, like the animal, leaving the woods, hunting only the fields and patches where the spikes and forkhorns, the "swamp rabbits," toddled along with the does. That was one of the feelings he remembered from her, and, frozen there, the hesitation overtook him, drawing him back to the previous fall at college when he had met her.

Maybe he was in love with her before he ever met her. In a way this was true, because she (a wraith, at first, that later grew and materialized into her form—her watery, hazel eyes, small, upturned nose, straight sandy hair, and small body) was in a frequent dream-fancy he would have in his college days when he was alone or thinking about the future, realizing how unfulfilling it was to "plug" (as he called it at the time) a girl one week and then go for a month with no one, repeating the same drunken patterns over and over. The dream would come to him especially on those evenings when he would be on the road at dusk. It haunted him as he drove back to his little house up at school, with the color draining into the west and the cold air whistling through the seams of the vents.

He would be with her in front of a fire, winter, in a small cabin. Staring at the throbbing embers, he would notice the sap hissing and bubbling from the end of the green oak — all wrapt in the fluttering flames, the secure, steamy sounds. It was almost as if the darkness coldly creeping towards the hearth was warded off, pushed back into the corners by the warmth and the glow. He would sit with her late into the night, sipping the straight bourbon on crushed ice, covered with the cast copper warmth of the fire, the murmur of softly spoken words, and the inner-glow of the whiskey. Then they would love with the darkness held in the corners of the room.

So when she appeared, when he first saw her that night at the fraternity, where the loud talk and drinking and blaring jukebox were irritating and intimidating and had been for a long time, she began to fill this space in front of the fire. The more he talked with her, the more he caught the moistness of her eye and the way her mouth opened when she smiled, the more he smelt her clean whiskey breath, the more real this dream began to be.

One of the things that excited him was her love for the outdoors, and he listened that night as she told of how she skied and camped, had even been hunting and skeet shooting with her father. Then they had compared their homes, South Carolina and Colorado, and he had been drawn into her world with the excitement one has in discovering new turf. He imagined the high mountains peaked with dry snow, the gorges and passes, the valleys with streams lush in the summer. All was exotic, rich, expansive. When he looked at her talking with the slight glow of pleasant reminiscence on her face, she, too, seemed to possess those qualities.

When she told him how much she thought of hunters and hunting (just after he had described his winters in the woods after deer and duck and quail), he noticed that she was interested in him. The realization was like the warm flash of a flame brushing his face, and then they went outside and talked quietly about the outdoor fires and camping in the crisp coldness, waking in sleeping bags. Through it all he started to say to himself, "This is the one, this is the one," excitedly, over and over until he was sure that she was saying it to herself, too.

The more he was with her, the more he realized that he was in love, that he was in the middle with it growing sumptuously around him. It was something he had never experienced before with such spontaneity, except when he was a child and used to watch his mother, under the hum and enveloping whiteness of the fluorescent light, cook Sunday supper for him, or when he would stand on the beach and watch his father fight a channel bass up and down the surf with his light spinner. At times, driving, after dropping her off at her apartment in the evenings, he would smile to himself with the music seeming to flow through his body, and say with a grin that grew with his word, "This is it, this is it."

But the hesitation came one evening when he was in her room, only an occasional car sputtering by. She clicked on the light and had gotten out of bed as he grabbed both pillows and propped them beneath his head. His eyes traced the smooth furrow of her spine to her buttocks.

He patted her lower back and she caught his hand and held it. Then she stretched out her arm, picking up a flannel wrapper from the chair, slinging it around her, and tying the sash in one fluid sweep.

"I'll be back," she said, and in the glow of the bedside

lamp, he focused on a black and white photo, low on the wall by her desk.

It was a shot of her on skis, leaning up on the poles planted in the ankle-deep powder, smiling with her face darkened, her hair blonde in relief, flowing. The clear focus seemed to make her look in place in the snow and sun. But as he leaned out of bed, he saw a dark-haired man in the background blurred in the haze of depth but still wide and powerful-looking. He could only make out a white smile on the broad face, but this person somehow seemed to be gazing at her. That was what made him stop, as if something inside had thrown a switch and generators were winding dismally to a halt.

When the door clicked shut, he swung around, pulling her close as she shed her robe. He switched off the light, and her hair dropped down over his face. She flicked it back, and as he saw the nebulous outline of her small nose, they were together, his tongue finding hers, the moist warmth seeming to start his pulse again.

"You know," he said. "I haven't, I mean I haven't ever . . . I've never loved and I'm realizing that, well . . ."

"What?" she said, her hand on her side of his face, caressing.

"I mean." He felt almost too vulnerable now. "I'm in love with you, big time, and, by God, I want you to tell me that if there's anyone else anywhere. I mean I'd better get up right now and leave because I'm sinking, GODDAMN, I mean, I don't want to get all googy-eyed and then have you run off . . ."

"No," she cut him off. "There was, but there isn't."

And then they were together.

As he looked at the thicket, he felt himself shudder. Its blocklike form materialized once again. Imagining a fallen sweetgum as a barrier placed there by the animal itself, his blood-flow refilled him. "Go," he said and then entered. Inside the passages and alleys were the signs of the rut too—the rubs bending the small trees as if the animal had been practicing, strengthening his neck and honing his horns in preparation for fight. Never had he seen such a beast. Following the network of gullied trails under the trees deeper, nervously fingering the trigger guard of the rifle, he came to where the trunks were wrapt and tangled with gray brambles and shriveling honeysuckle vines. There was a strange opening in them.

At first he really didn't know what it was at all. Rocking his head from side to side, he squatted, finding the prints leading in and out—a tunnel! Then, dropping to his knees, he entered, pushing onto his stomach and snaking as the animal had. There were no more tracks, only bare spots and long streaks, where the knobs of the deer's knees had scuffed the dirt. In the middle, he stopped, half-winded from the crawling but fueled by an intense curiosity. He could visualize the beast: first dropping to its knees, front and head bowing and hooking the antlers into the thick mat, then pushing, tearing, thrusting the neck back and forth, prodding its way through.

In all there were some twenty-five yards of tunnel. Near the end, it banked to the right, and during that stretch he stopped often, pulling off the barren blackberry vines as they raked across his hat and back, clawing, stinging his hands like nettles. Finally it opened into a small glade of tan wiregrass. He stood and saw the mashed pockets where the buck bedded and could bask in the open sun without fear. Stooping, his gun across his knees, he laid his hand on the spot, and it seemed to radiate a presence: a vague warmth. It was then, there, as he rose and looked at the morning sun streaming through the ground mists, that he said, "I have to have it, I have to hunt it." There were no Becauses or Reasons, just those words, and he turned, leaving the woods until evening.

. . . . .

Having stopped only once to put his tree stand in an oak on the edge of the swamp, he sits in the thicket now. His back against the base of the pine, full shade and sooty trunks, a yellow-brown cast beckons quietly off the fallen needles. It seems as if some supernatural radiance glows from below as well as above. The cool October noon around him now, it is hard to imagine the heat and dusk and anger of late summer and September. All of that is distant, and even the flakes of bark no longer pick at his back. All control of his muscles is gone, melting into the tree, the very core of it. The rifle across his legs feels as if it is slowly sinking through the faded denim, merging with the flesh of his upper thighs and the bone below.

He wants the buck to move now, to come horizontally and like a gray-black ghost against the straight bases of the pines, to float into his scope without sound, dipping its head and antlers under the low limbs and meshing overhang, cloven hooves piercing the forest floor. Almost dozing, he dreams it, painlessly, easily, the animal drifting steadily; and with the same confluence, he raises the rifle, mashing the trigger: explosion without sound, the bullet kissing the shoulder, killing swiftly, without blood. His.

The two and a half weeks after the letter until now, he remembers only as a haze, a drained haze, where all the anger welled and clouded until there was nothing but sleep. Lord, he slept those days, not caring about work on the farm. Then the next day he'd get up and drive the tractor, harrowing until dark, falling into bed again, overlooking the opening of deer season, just wanting time to pass, alone, with the gray light coming in through the closed blinds, the stale smell of sleep settling down like dust.

But now he questions and feels the hints of tension inside, the tension that riddled him during the summer. Perhaps it was like the screwworm that his father once told him of and how that pest nearly wiped out all the deer in the Southeast in a summer's time. The adult flies would swarm around a deer with a flesh wound or a doe that had just dropped a fawn, or the eyes of the fawns themselves. In these sores the female fly would lay her eggs deep into the wound. Then, after the scab had formed, with the skin close to healing, the eggs would hatch. The larvae would begin to eat their way out, reopening the cut, at the same time boring and spreading into the animal until they weakened it and killed it as slowly as maggots passing through carrion.

In the room that night with the picture on the wall and then the love that he felt as they stayed until morning, the larvae had been planted.

But there were the good times. They are what make him cringe now as he hunts in the thicket, wanting the deer to come, wanting to focus and listen for the faint steps in the straw or the cracking of a stick.

. . .

For the rest of the fall, the winter, and the beginning of spring, they lived. Never had he felt such energy. It was crazy energy. In the afternoons he would run in the country for miles, and smelling the earth again as it thawed and softened, he would find the suitable pace, letting the ends of his fingers flick freely and click a rhythm into his head—over and over, with his lungs loosened, the movement of the blood numbing any kind of pain. In the evenings they would study or go to the café and listen to jazz and drink wine or cook out.

Sometimes while they worked he would stop and watch her reading, the hair covering all but the hints of tan and freckles on her forehead. After a few minutes she would look up. At first, a bewildered expression would come upon her face, like waking and not knowing which room or even house you are in, then a smile and laugh would spread and come out softly. He would always have to put down his work and go over and kiss and hold her as if the mere touch were essential, like the recharging of an electric cell within, prone to falter without a source of power.

But as spring came full, with the end of school in sight, the pain started. It made it so he couldn't eat. More and more he had to have her with him, alone. Sometimes even the presence of his roommate, Odell, with whom he'd grown up and schooled all of his life in South Carolina, and who was almost married to a girl down there, would make him feel jumpy. When Odell talked with her, and they would laugh, he would rock in his chair, blurt a short cackle and then jump up, grabbing her hand and saying, "Come on, you've got to see this new fishing hole I found over at Bolson's Lake."

Parties were worse, even though they were small and consisted of friends he'd known for all four years at school. He would have to stay at her side, touch her. Talking quickly, crunching the ice of his drink, he found himself cutting down people with bitter jokes for no reason at all. Then, only a minute later, when she was at the other side of the room, he would feel miserably vulnerable.

It seemed each night they would leave the parties earlier. He drove his truck fast down the roads, the suspension bumping and rattling over the frost heaves that winter's ice had planted there. Only at his house, in his room, in the bed and darkness would his pulse level, and he would repeat, again and again, his love for her.

Two weeks before school ended, on their way to a graduation party, he turned the truck and took her to the lake, saying nothing until they arrived. They got out and ambled down to the edge, where the moon had risen and reflected in the center of the tapering tips of the trees.

"What about it?" He pulled on her.

"It's pretty out here," she said, nestling her head between his neck and shoulder.

"What about the summer?" he said as he gazed at the water and saw the top of his head mirrored there.

"I'm not looking forward to it."

"I'm not either."

They laughed, and then the tension spread in his lower stomach and up into his throat; and it seemed as if the weight of her head on him, her body pressed against his side, compounded it.

"When are you going to come and see me? You know I'm going to get kind of tired of staring at row markers and sucking dust on tractors. . . . I worry about you by yourself out there."

There was a silence.

"Oh, I'm all right by myself out there; it's home."

The two words cut him like an axe thrown into his chest.

"But if I get that job right when I get back, and work for a couple of months, August would be good," she said.

Yeah, he thought, then said it. A cool shudder came up the back of his neck, quelling the hurt of the blow. "The first of August?"

She nodded.

"Jesus!" He threw his head back. "When you get off that plane, I'm gonna romp and stomp and raise hell. We'll go to the beaches. Hell, you've never seen beaches like the ones on the sea isles, beaches that stretch for miles with nobody. We'll fish . . . "

"You know what?" She seemed excited, too. "I'm going to make you a quilt."

It is amazing the power that fills you when you start to dream, when you create something in your head and convince yourself that you're going to get to it, to have it. The means, the time spent attaining it are nothing. Your eyes water and your heart rumbles. Your breaths come in clear. Gathering momentum, you want to scream, run headlong into anything, bat your head against the trees. All fear and infirmities and doubts of self are converted internally, then consumed as energy sweeping through your body.

His eyes cloud the passages and alleys that stretch before him in the thicket. He looks up and squints at the sun squeezing through the trees, pupils contracting tightly. "Hunt," he says. "Goddammit, hunt." And with the first movement, the tight movement he conditions himself for, whenever he is swallowed in by the woods and goes after deer, cold sparks jump in his legs, the blood finding passage, then gradually thawing the tingle. Pushing up, joints and back stiff from the sitting, he feels sort of confused in the thicket, confined with the early afternoon light showering overhead, dissolved through the tops of the trees, sifting slowly downwards onto the fallen needles. It really isn't good hunting here on the ground anyway; and even though he has tried to mask his scent by rubbing the sappy juices of crushed pine tops on his clothes and exposed skin, he knows the animal will smell or see him. It is peaceful in a way, almost intoxicating, but he must move, come out of it.

Picking up the rifle, he walks, his glance moving from his feet to the opening ahead, checking the twigs, rocking into each step. The sun bends down west. Without watch time, without time at all, he knows he must work at it now. As he stalks out of the swamp bottom he repeats, "Concentrate and hunt," with each placed step.

His portable stand is already out at the edge, high in the crotch of a sprawling laurel oak. It overlooks the trail from the thicket and is best to hunt in either the early mornings or late afternoons, those cool edges of day when animals move from their beds and feed, lured by the acorns and the browse of the second growth forests, the remnants of crops in the fields beyond.

From his vantage now, he sees everything, checking for the landmarks—the trail that runs out of the swamp, then parallels it on the slight incline where the timeless woods of the hardwood bottom bank up and, suddenly, on the other side of the firebreak become manwoods, the planted loblolly and slash pines, thinned and lined as crops with the wiregrass bristling below. Through the trees which he faces, the sun hovers coolly over a distant hedgerow. He snaps away the branches that obscure vision and checks his braces through them.

Now he listens to the breaths and movements of the swamp behind him, every so often cornering his eyes towards the lone trail and catching the colors there, aflame, the deciduous fire of autumn—the yellows of the poplars, high-topped orange of the cypresses, burnt and crackly brown of the oaks, and the yellow-greens that linger in the honeysuckle.

There is something, a quietness, a hollowness that seems soothing in that swamp. It emanates and spreads around him. Maybe that was it. The thought startles him. The swamps.

One weekend in spring, he took her home to meet his parents and see the farm. On the road, just as the maples were beginning to blossom, the new buds like red mist around the limbs, the farmers were beginning to turn land. In the late of those evenings, they burned windrows, and the cool, earth air mingled with the smoke buoyed and hanging in white strips across the road. While they drove, and the sun set, they began to enter the swamps as the land flattened and bottomed on either side of the highway. Great cypresses dwarfed the other trees, and an occasional pair of summer ducks would skitter right above them.

"Look, woodies!" He swerved slightly, leaning over her, watching the birds as far as he could until they pitched or disappeared.

She gazed at him, then almost pressed her small nose against the window, staring at the thick woods. Now the trees darkened into a solid wall, only small slithers of color mirrored in the swampy waters of meandering branches.

First with a grin, then a forced shudder, she twisted her face. "This place gives me the creeps. Where are all the slimy swamp monsters?"

He talked, hissing lowly, "They only come out at midnight," and went on making up stories of how late night travelers—cars, buses, even eighteen-wheeled trucks —were inhaled by the massive, snotty blobs hanging across the roads and river branches.

On the serious level, however, the one that is always feeling the truth in your head no matter what you say or do, he never thought of his country in any way but benevolently. There was no horror. To him all was as soft and as peaceful and as friendly and as steady as anything he could ever think of. Even in times when he felt frustrated or nervous, he would turn to the mental pictures of the Low-country for consolation. Picturing a stable live oak, moss laden and standing alone in a flat field, he would experience, at first, a strange mixture of sorrow, loneliness, solitude, and then, his eyes almost watering, he would always derive a special kind of strength and comfort.

Maybe she spooked, he thought. A flash of a snowy mountain, steep and jagged, hit him, making him grip the wood and blued metal of the rifle. "Hunt," he says again, as if the word is a desperate alternative.

The coldness now slithers from the bottom of the swamp, and he feels it seeping upwards, almost as if the chill lives and like an animal moves forward cautiously, slinking from its retreat in the waning wake of the sun. Soon he will be able to see his breath coming out in front, but now he only feels the chill pinching the edges of his crusted socks, nipping his ears and the fingers that cradle the gun. Now in the tree he loses himself, and only feeling transparent, like an apparition of tuned and toned senses, he synchronizes with the forest around. A leaf lofts from above, spiraling downwards, then batted up, swirling and tumbling on the currents, scratching the branches, finally flashing as it chinks on the ground. The moon, full and rising in the south, resplendent even in the late afternoon sky, rivals the retreating sun. "Yes, the moon." He eyes it, remembering it from the night before, the first day with the deer. "The moon."

. . . . .

From the same tree he sat late and into the night. After dusk the light never really left the swamp. It only shifted its casts. The fire of sunset bloomed into silver moon color, shadows of the trees etched on the ground. He was about to get down, to return to the truck and then the cabin, but a deer bleated from the swamp, and he keyed on it, turning slowly, the cautious cadence of walking animals following. In the same instant an owl, perched high in the tree next to him, hooted back into the swamp, the trilling cutting the night air, traveling like a powerful wedge, then spreading out into the thickness beyond. The deer stopped, and he looked up at the bird: a perfect stony shadow balanced on the limbs. He knew the animals hadn't spooked, though, and after the owl sounded three or four more times, they started again, coming close enough so he could feel their presence below him. They paused, and this time he knew it was his presence they felt.

His stomach wound tight. For an instant he wanted to jump or scream out into the air as the owl had done. He shivered the impulse away, waiting, listening, feeling for the next move . . . and it came, crackly on the leaves under his tree, the lead doe stopped twenty yards away, scratching, tamping the mulch-dirt, trying to make the sensed danger show itself. He held, and then the animal weaved. He could see it, a nebulous shadow, tapping the dirt with its front legs, the weight shifting from foot to foot in a drawn out intrinsic dance, the rhythm, lightly pawed.

As mysteriously as it had started, the jig was over. He could see two of them, small does, walking out of the shadows and into the strong silver of the moon, by the trunk of his tree and out past him, heads bobbing backwards as they bucked the incline to the planted pines. He'll follow, he thought to himself, hoping, keeping his eyes on the two deer as they moved in and out of the light in the direction of the fields.

Then there was no cold or sound, vapid, like the color which had seeped out of the woods with the setting sun. Blood rushed through his head, swishing and pulsing in his temples. A weakness seemed to flutter up his legs. In the moonlight, quietly seething in the mossy branches of the tree, a spreading spirit emanated from the bowels of the swamp, reaching him an instant before he could hear it, brushing his face like a charged piece of silk and taking the breath out of his lungs. The buck walked towards him; the unscared and unhurried, pointed walk with the does having already scouted his path for him.

Focusing on the sound, he squeezed the safety off and waited. But then he realized that his whole body was quavering. The joggling of blood filled his head and muffled the footsteps. Frantically, he searched, opening his eyes as wide as he could, trying to gather more light. But no sooner than it had come, it was gone, way out past him in the pines. He heard the crack of a twig, saw the silver flash of a flank, and then all was swallowed into the night beyond.

He had sat for quite a while, calming himself, trying to figure out how the buck had done it, how it had passed so close without baring itself. It made him dizzy. The animal was like a spirit that walked on the shafts of light. Maybe he was hunting something that was unreal, and all this time in the forest was futile. How could he have steadied and squeezed off, shaking as he was? He snapped the gun back on safe. Slinging it over his shoulder, propping up in order to release his stand and climb down, he scanned once more, hoping to catch another quicksilver flash or trace the outline of a blocky figure. Then he knew what had happened, and it caused him to sink back down on the platform and just sit. The buck had moved in the shadows. It had skirted so closely, right behind the does, but following the imperfect circles and inky splotches on the ground. He had seen that lead deer come out and walk illuminated by the hue of the moon, and when he had heard the buck, he had expected to see it in the same bright pools. It had merely hugged the shade, slipped carefully past.

.   .   .   .   .

"You learn." He is watching the sun, orange-brown, burst red as it singes the top of the distant hedgerow past the pines. Hot bands of pink cirrus hang high in the west as if in formation; livid birds of prey, taut against the winds of the jetstream. He begins to think about Colorado, and he grips the stand under him as if something is going to tear him from the woods. "Leave the summer sunsets, they're gone." For a second he sees only her head, then the image dissolves.

A squirrel barks from behind. He swings, finding it pointed towards the ground, frozen silently on the base of a swamp poplar. It talks again, "chit-chit-churr," and the bark looks as if it flits up the tail with every chirp. In a quick bound, it plops to the ground, burrows and grubs in the leaves, coming up with an acorn, poised. Its tail flutters then furls along its back like a coat. All of its sounds are light on the ground, in the leaves, not like the piercing, pointed walk of deer. Then the squirrel rustles its head towards the swamp, freezes and bounces to the tree, barking and clattering off into the branches: a sign.

He focuses on the deer trail now, scoping for movement. All is mute: the deep, almost limitless tree trunks. Somewhere from the bottom of it all, a piliated woodpecker trills in sets of three, then drums loudly on a hollow.

With the first crack, he knows it. Then there's another, followed by the expansive, seeping quiet of the bed. *He knows it.* His heart begins to rap wildly, the flow through his temples. As light as a warm wind, the spirit-feeling comes, and then there is the distinct walk through the leaves. Alone, it moves, and he swings only his head to the side, picks a spot to watch the edge of the swamp, and waits. With another cold snap, the hair on the back of his head bristles. His eyes water. The buck is there, finer than any picture or imagining that's come before; immobile, standing as if it had materialized from nothing or sprouted instantly from the ground, solid, chiseled, bold. The squat legs support its heavy chest and long, powerful flanks. Sideways, the neck bulges thick with white—the sign of age, of seasons survived. A similar shade of gray circles the muzzle and wise, amber eyes. And the antlers spread out past cocked ears, as big around at the base as a pistol handle, long tines curving up in perfect symmetry.

Then it moves, seeming to step on a transparent plane an inch above the ground, muscles rippling in the flank and shoulder. Bowing its neck, the head and rack slanting under a myrtle, it moves out of the swamp.

Just before it crosses the firebreak, he remembers the gun and with trembling arms raises it. Erect, he finds the animal in the scope, which pulls the image into a closer, encircled world. Concentrating, he steadies, precisely X-ing the animal's shoulder blade with the crosshair, and then stops. With the red haze of sky behind it, the buck turns its head towards the swamp, and he doesn't see it looking at him. He only draws a full breath and on the exhalation starts squeezing the trigger, tightening ever so slightly, peering intently through the X to that spot on the shoulder, the patch of coat, and flesh below.

The rifle bellows, hurling the soft-nosed bullet out in front of a quick orange flame, clubbing the animal's shoulder, buckling it to its knees. With the sound still rolling, searing fresh through the humid air, the deer scampers to its feet and runs. He finds it through the scope again, pursuing it, almost panicking, his head boiling. Swinging, he squeezes again and again, three more times, and on the third, the buck starts to topple with the reports echoing out and wailing on one another. It hits the dirt of the firelane, scuffing up a small puff of dust, kicking twice, dead.

Then he's on the ground, not knowing how he got out of the tree, the bluish haze of burnt powder clearing. Still frenzied, he runs in the moonlit dusk to the deer and then, as if he doesn't see it, to the spot where he first shot at it. With his chest bucking under erratic breaths, he stops, eyeing the splattering of blood on the dirt; the foamy, bubble-flecked lung blood, black until he fingers it and brings it up in front of his face. By the time he's walked the trail to where the buck fell, he realizes that something has gone lax. He breathes smoothly as if something left him, traveling through the rifle and out with the sound.

"I've killed it, I've killed it." Now he sees, looking down at the magnificent animal, the head tilted slightly downwards following the incline of the swamp fringe, massive antlers poking the earth. The body is full, the white underbelly almost glowing. There are four holes grouped around its shoulder, matting the black hair. One would have killed it.

He lays his gun down beside the buck and realizes that

the gun is his humility, and he can neither feel overly proud or even capable because of it, only thankful. He finds the knife on his belt, takes a sharpening steel from his pocket and crouches slowly by the kill. On his knees, he strops the knife against the steel, facing the luminous line of horizon.

He gives thanks, not directing gratitude toward anything (although his eyes never leave the buck), letting the thoughts, the words disperse into the forest.

With the last stroke, he thumbs the blade, then rakes it across the top of his hand, flaying the hair into a neat pile. He turns and with his free hand rolls the deer on its back. Its legs open, and he is on it, straddling the huge chest. Rubbing the high stomach, where the ribs converge over the diaphragm, he feels the warmth still under the sleek winter coat. He slits the animal's belly, running his fingers under the skin, ahead of the knife, raising it so the blade won't puncture the organs below, making his own careful hole. And then he enters with the warmth of the entrails and hot blood, slick and wet on his hands and forearms, the pungent, almost rank inner smell steaming into the air. It is as if the essence of the animal drafts up into his face. He savors it, is deep in it, and then feels it pass out into the woods around, cooling, gone.

After he removes the diaphragm, he reaches into the

cavity, severing the windpipe and jugular. Just before pulling the insides onto the earth beside him, he glances at the head. He studies the proportioned features — the wide-brown sentient eyes, whitened muzzle, stable rack, and muscle-packed neck.

With a fluid sweep he rakes the entrails out onto the dirt that absorbs the liquids as the carcass drains. He finds a stick and wedges it between the two halves of the rib cage so the meat will cool, then stoops, powdering his hands in the loose soil to dry the blood. Picking up the rifle, then grabbing it by the antlers, he starts pulling. He has only a quarter mile to go before he comes out of the woods. The dead animal is his, in a way she never could have been.

NIGHT CASTING

When I was twelve years old and August afternoons were spent struggling through summer reading lists, we would shrimp at night. At that point — a time in which passions were held by the movement of the tides, the creatures of the marsh — it was the only way we could rationalize the afternoon rest periods which our mothers still made us endure. We were quite positive that they had no idea about us now. All those books, those *Penrod*s and *Red Pony*s, were simply meaningless if not idiotic. No, we were becoming what we fancied ourselves to be forever—watermen. Our muscles, bunching at the shoulders, could handle the nets and the oars; and neither the heat of a midday sun nor the dark of a full night could keep us still.

I would go with Sumner, who was tall and rangy but had the long biceps and breadth of shoulder to throw a six-foot net for hours. Sometimes he looked ridiculous on the casting platform as he grappled with the huge net. But once he had measured and collected the folds, placed the hem-rope between his teeth, an unbelievable sense of command would cut from his eye. At that very instant, all his timing, concentration, and experience seemed to coalesce. Then, with an almost lackadaisical flick of his torso, he would spin the net out across the water, right where he wanted it. To this day, I believe Sumner took more from the river in a physical sense than I. There were times, as he moved quickly around the boat, rising to pole into a creek or slinging a line to a dock, when his long sunburned limbs would curve, luff like the arcs of a net thrown into an afternoon's breeze.

Sumner had learned how to make the nets, too. He would sit on the bluff in the shade of a massive loblolly and squint down the river, brushing his strokes and knots impatiently, unevenly. Many times, as I watched him, I would think of how different his strokes were from Moderator's, even though Sumner coveted the old man's. I attributed that difference to the difference in their ages.

Maybe it's time I talked about Moderator, the old fisherman. (Yes, that was really his name.) After all, without him, both of us would have known very little or nothing about the making of nets or the catching of shrimp—or about the river itself.

I guess I was the first one to discover him. I take that back; it was my mother who took me to him. A shy ten years of age, I remember looking up at the old man on the porch of his simple house from the back seat of my mother's station wagon. With his black mustache covering a slightly cleft lip; his wide, tobacco-runny eyes; the low and powerful body, hitching slightly to the side as he walked, initially he brought to mind a walrus I'd seen in some animated picturebook.

Mom would buy shrimp, crabs, sometimes croakers and trout from him. He kept his catch in a galvanized washtub with crushed ice and a cool piece of burlap covering them. The fish would have fresh, clear eyes, and I remember the smell of the wetted newspaper he'd wrap them in. Occasionally Mom would bring him an old suit or shirt or pair of shoes from my father. It's odd that I never thought he looked funny out there in those light flannel or pinstriped Brooks Brothers suits. There would always be smears of mud on the trousers. The jackets, sleeves rolled to the elbow, would be worn as a shirt over his bare chest, and he would tie strings high on his ankles to keep the cuffs out of the water when he cast in his boat. (Later, after we got to know him, he told us this practice of tying strings gave him strength on the river.) Maybe it was because I was in awe of him that I didn't think he was funny. There was a powerful order and a rustic dignity to the man. You could tell that he knew they were good clothes that were given to him. He planned to make them last as long as his profession would allow.

When we were old enough to ride the shady mile of white clay road to his house on our bikes, and our interest in the things he caught overcame our shyness, we would go to him in the late evenings and sit on his porch or stand under the palmetto where he worked on his nets. It was the time of day that was too pretty for reticence. Our uneasiness magically dissolved in the throbbing sheen of cicadae, their sound bringing both night and coolness onto the trees, the house, the dirt. Slowly the stories came, mixed with quiet lessons as we helped him head shrimp or watched him patch a net. His voice became addictive balm, flour-smooth, like the gray dirt of his yard under our bare feet.

Late one June afternoon he did something that surprised us. He made us both bracelets, "charms," he called them. Patiently, firmly, and with odd determination, he braided the nylon net cord onto our narrow wrists. A day after that, he asked us to go on the boat with him and learn, "help out."

During that first summer of fishing with him, our bracelets changed. The brackish and slow water, the sun, the sweat, the mud of moonless nights grayed them, frayed them down to the weary, the old, the almost stoic hue of weathered cypress. When we asked him for new, shiny ones, he'd flatly refused, saying, "Dey still strong."

And now, thinking back to that time in life, that age in time, it was as if the bracelets were emblems, not of the river itself or even our tutelage on it, but of what the river would do, year after year, quiet tide after tide, to one's soul—if one were calm and respectful enough to let it. And I can't help thinking that even Moderator had placed them on us as just that—symbols—not only because he held a Low-country waterman's respect for superstition, but because he was sensible.

The last time we saw Moderator was at night, that impatient summer when we were twelve. Things had changed somewhat from the two years before. Now we were old enough to shrimp at night. We no longer went in his boat as helpers but met him out on the river in Sumner's bateau, with our own nets. Our wrists had finally outgrown the bracelets.

But the most important change was not with us, but with the river—it was no longer all ours. It had been invaded by a number of agile power skiffs which pulled thirty-foot drag nets and which, in a single night, could sweep more out of the channels and holes than what Moderator could catch in a week. Their presence had made the old man noticeably more quiet, and as the summer progressed they seemed to sap his strength. There were many times when a wide and confused look would wobble onto his face instead of the steady, honest, and squinty expression he normally met the river and marsh with.

Although first interested by rumors of their huge catches, it didn't take us long to develop a strong disdain for these new people and their noisy boats. I must admit that one afternoon we pulled up to a skiff that had just completed its drag and gaped at the mountains of shrimp rising about the seats, almost to the gunwale. We wondered how in the world the one shrimper would head all those shrimp. The man who ran the boat was too busy to answer our questions. He had puffy eyes and a chest like a barrel and wore a yellow slicker that looked like overalls. His white rubber boots were slick and we could see him crushing shrimp in the bottom of the boat as he moved around, jerking the net's doors out of the water and banging them onto the side of the boat.

At the time we had no idea why these new people and their loud fiberglass skiffs had suddenly appeared. Rumor had it they came from the subdivisions that were cropping up on the west side of town. It was not until twenty years later, when I was at a noisy sales convention in Detroit and they served some pinkish goo called "Shrimp Savannah," that I finally sensed the true magnitude of change that had started on our river in those innocent years. Looking around me at the scores of people my age, both white and black (though for some reason hardly distinguishable in our pinstriped suits bought on credit from J. C. Penney), I felt that the same latent mechanism that had thrown us all together in that Midwestern city and allowed us to eat the deveined fragments of supposedly East Coast shrimp (out of season, no less), that very same immense force had robbed us of our river all those years ago. But I'm getting away from my story—account, rather—of the two of us and that old man, casting on his river that last night.

It was a spring tide of no moon when the river was quiet in its ebb, dark as a wolf's throat. I walked down along the

bluff to Sumner's house, listening keenly for the two important sounds—the distant engines of the skiffs or the sandy
steady chafe and lap of oars.

Sumner was there on his dock in the floodlight. He
collected buckets, scurried to the lockbox in squeaky
sneakers, drew up the nets, which brushed the side of the
bateau in an excited rap. I could tell he heard me as I
approached, and without looking up he cranked up the
small Evinrude with one hand, a puff of smoke, white,
clouding like steam around his head, then blue and out
into the dark, downriver.

"You got everything?" I said, dropping my net onto the
casting platform. Then I uncleated the bow line, ready to
cast off.

"Might need an extra cooler," he said, hesitating, and I
could sense the mild superstition of overconfidence holding him back. No doubt it came from Moderator, who was
probably already somewhere out in the dark.

"We don't need it. Come on," he said finally. "Let's find
the old man."

I pushed the boat from the slip, hearing the light engine
click into reverse like a cricket trying to clear its throat.

If the skiffs were dragging, Moderator had stopped showing up. Maybe he would come, but we could never find
him. We often thought that he was probably up some deep

turn of a creek, sitting in the dark without his lantern lit, picking at the side of his worn craft with those long fingers of his, trying to figure things out. Then again, maybe he already had it figured out. But we knew he would be there that night. The tide, in its spring, was too low to allow the skiffs to pass the bars and oyster rakes of the creek.

We cut our small engine well before the first shrimping creek and rowed. There was a mysterious quiet coating the river like a film. It made us — no, coerced us — upriver, even though the rowing was difficult against the slight ebb.

I didn't have the patience or strength of wrist to push-row like Moderator, so I faced the stern, looking over my shoulder every third or fourth pull for a cluster of myrtles that marked the mouth of the creek. As I started to veer, Sumner guiding me around the bar, we saw the old man's lamp flutter on. Then his net crashed on the water like a blast of steam on a cold winter's night. The two things — the sight and the sound — were our signal. I turned and rose with a single oar to pole and paddle, while Sumner lit our lantern and began casting from the bow.

With each cast, I could feel the warm water flick onto my face from the net, taste the tarnish of the muddy water mixing with my sweat.

"It's good tonight," Sumner said.

I knew he'd hit a good hole and was feeling the vibration of the trapped shrimp through the cord. Then he spat through his teeth like a barnacle. Crouching and leaning slightly into it, he began to retrieve the net with the tight, hooking cuts of a boxer. Finally pulling it up in front of him, he spread the radius the way a young girl would display a new dress to her mother. Then, quite violently, he shook it, the shrimp falling like gray rain, flicking and darting, finding the water and quietly shivering and walking awkwardly in the flat dark of the bottom of the boat.

Our slow yet thorough weave up the creek, drawn by Sumner's net, quietly prodded by my oar, took us closer to the old man, who moved by himself, by his strong net alone. Even though we were now taking great amounts of prime, white shrimp, there was something that made us want to hurry and catch Moderator. Maybe there was even a slight jealousy of him, his perfectly timed and patient casts, his simple dark skin and dark bateau blending with the walls of fertile mud behind him. And, strange, you could even say we wanted to be old like him. But we remembered to take our time, to fish the creek seriously and thoughtfully, to pay attention to what was around us, as he'd taught us to do.

More than halfway up, we stirred a school of mullet in the flats. Bunching, turning, they became confused, and instead of fleeing, rocketed toward our light in a clatter.

Most of them hit the gunwale, bouncing back like small torpedoes. A few, however, cleared it and landed in the well, where they disrupted the shrimp. I pounced on them and put them in the cooler where they batted and flapped and shivered.

By the time we reached the first fork, Moderator was sitting in his boat, quietly studying Sumner's final casts. After the last retrieve, Sumner shucked the net cord from his wrist, turned and sat up front, scooping a handful of shrimp to head. The boat, barely moving from the cast, nudged Moderator's bateau. He slowly reached over, grabbed the gunwale and tethered us, oarlock to oarlock, with a piece of cord.

Almost immediately, we both noticed his silence and seriousness, even though a mist of easiness and kindness could never leave his eyes. I guess he seemed a bit awkward, for usually he would have already started some speculation or anecdote or lesson. There in the flicking, breathless lamplight, the tall walls of mud and marsh and darkness high around us, Moderator, for an instant, began to look really old, shriveled, even maybe scared. He rolled his yellow eyes to the side, massed his chest quickly as if gasping, and squirmed as if something inside of him was about to choke him. After a considerable silence, he forced himself to speak.

"You go through them mullets this evening?"

We nodded, relieved to hear his voice.

"Had a few jump in the boat," I said.

"Yeah," he looked up. "I gots a couple, too. Thing hop up in the light, like to buss me up side the head." He finally gave a little chuckle. "Old people say when fish jump in the boat, he bring he luck with him." Then Moderator sort of grunted, suddenly falling silent as before. Musing, he twisted his head and sullenly said, "Some a dem old Geechee fishermen say he bring bad luck, though. Say he in a place he not 'spose to be."

Once again the old man fell silent and restless like before. The worry, so unnatural to his every pore, stuck out on his face like a mask of sorts.

"Maybe old man's sign don't make no matter, anyways. Ain't nobody gonna listen at them." He gave a melodramatic sort of sigh, glancing at the bottom of his boat, then sheepishly at us.

Both of us still looked at him unflaggingly, still open and trusting. We looked at him with the same interest and awe we had from the beginning, the same thirst we had when he first showed us how to cast, to read the channel of a creek, to fish for sheepshead under pilings, with fiddler crabs. And maybe at that point, he noticed us, noticed that we were still there along with the sheltering calm of the low tide. We were there with him in our patient and small bateau. We were not closed up in an air-conditioned house lying in front of a TV set, eating chips from plastic bags. We were there, with him, on the quiet river, still ready to learn more.

A small puff of breeze stirred the marsh above us. Somewhere out at the mouth of the sound, the tide was starting to turn. Still looking thoughtfully at us, Moderator perked his head up and sniffed. All of a sudden all the awkwardness and tension fell from his features, quickly replaced by his squinty smile. You could see a comforting shiver course through his old frame, bringing new light to his eye, a new and now-permanent confidence. Then he was in motion, excited.

"Ain't never done this before, but I'm gonna." He reached under the bow and brought out a dark cedar box twice the size of a car battery. We had never seen it before, but immediately knew it was something special from the way he handled it. Putting it on the seat beside him, he opened it from the top and pulled out a square piece of blackened tin, placing it on the heading board in front of him.

Sumner and I gave each other questioning glances. But Moderator was now quite busy, as determined as he had been when he put the bracelets on us two years before.

Starting to hum softly, he pulled out an old coffee can next. There were a number of holes punched through the top, and two openings the size of your fist cut into either side of the bottom.

He must be going crazy, we both told ourselves with our eyes. The thought of making an excuse to leave at that point crossed my mind.

Finally he pulled a small frying pan from the box and placed it on top of the can. From a paper sack, he sprinkled charcoal and chips of fat-lighter in the little door. He lit them.

"A grill!" Sumner blurted in marvelously excited innocence. All of a sudden the magnificent idea caught me and I joined in. Hopping on our seats like robins on a lawn, we both began to sing it again and again, "A grill . . . a grill . . ."

The old man just smiled and reached down in the bottom of his boat and came up with a mullet.

"In all my years, ain't never eaten with white folks before," he said, leaning towards us almost cautiously. "But you my boys. And it's different out here . . . an this something . . ." he searched for words. "This something . . ." He finally just shook his head, leaving us with it.

He killed the fish by rapping their flat heads with the

weighted end of his knife, and you could see death passing neatly through them in a quiver. He scaled, then washed them in the creek water, finally cutting off the heads and throwing them in his crab bait basket. In a matter of minutes, he headed and peeled some two dozen prime prawns to go along with the mullet.

By then, the last whiffs of pine resin were in the smoke. The old man pulled a small jar of bacon grease from the box and dabbed some into the hot pan with the end of his knife.

"That's all the seasonings these fish needs out here," he said in a watery tone, laying the mullet, tails first, into the sputtering grease.

Almost instantly with the breeze, the river came alive with the smell. The old man, amber in the warm glow of both lantern and stove, turned the fish and stirred the shrimp. After he finished, he tore a paper bag into three pieces, and on each of the small squares he carefully placed a fish, sprinkling a handful of shrimp on top. He removed his hat, said a silent prayer, and then we ate.

The taste of those fish and shrimp isn't convertible to words or even phrases. Maybe the care with which Moderator sucked the last white flecks of meat from the backbone of his mullet can convey something.

It's hard to measure the time we sat in silence after we ate. No one uttered a sound, no one even looked at each other. Occasionally we could hear a faint rustle of a marsh wren shifting in its nest or a mullet plop out in the distant channel. Once we even heard the comforting blowing sigh of a porpoise making its way upriver to feed in our creeks.

Finally Moderator looked back towards the black mouth of the creek. He squinted hard at it and this was the same squint that had led him all his life. Then he began putting away his grill.

We followed his lead. Washing our hands over the side, we bailed the boat and scooped our shrimp into the cooler. Everything we did was unusually slow, as if we were cramped with sleep. About that time I realized that the tide was coming in quickly. It would soon let the skiffs over the bars.

Quite suddenly and still without a word, the old man untethered our small craft and we began to drift apart. He pulled his old andiron anchor from the mud and stood up slowly, starting his slow cast out.

We let him get a ways ahead of us before starting. And all of that time we mindlessly watched the languid, unflagging casts, the fluid circuit that joined him with the river. At last I found my net and stepped to the platform, still looking at him fluttering away as if in a dream.

Then, as if someone had grabbed our ears and twisted them, we heard the wailing of two skiffs, coarse, louder, cavitating as they made the turns upriver. Like a chain saw, the noise cut that thin thread of sound that was the old man's net on the water ahead of us.

Taking up an oar, Sumner moved to the back of the boat to pole, grimacing, looking down. Finally, with a faint, almost electrical weakness in my legs, I took up the net to cast, placing the hem in my teeth as he'd taught me, tasting the mud and salt and net of his river.

CATCHING THE MEANING

I'd come all the
way down the
coast to tell him.
Yet that afternoon I
remained silent as
we drove to the dock
at our cottage on the
river. He didn't talk,
either, and that was
beginning to frighten
me. I looked at him.
He had grown older,
weaker. His eyes protruded as if thick oil had been poured
into them. His skin was almost the color of raw prawns.

Maybe getting out in the sun will help him, I thought to
myself, and decided to keep my eyes on the road. I began

to think of how we used to fish ten years before when I was a teenager, and he would have to pull me out of bed and feed me Cokes and coffee to quell the hangovers, which came every night on those youthful weekends. Chuckling, he would fan his runny eggs in front of my nose. "How about some of these, too?" Then I'd feel his warm hand on my shoulder, and he'd say, "Go get the baits, I've got everything else down there." I would stumble outside, gagging until sweat beaded on my forehead, then sort through the various frozen fish, grab the tackle, and clop to the boat in untied sneakers.

It was big fishing then. Gas was only twenty-five cents a gallon and there seemed to be a limitless supply of it. We would run sixty miles to the Gulf Stream in a converted ocean racer that cruised at thirty-five knots and cut the seas like a forged harpoon. He was in love with the boat and would always steer standing for the whole two and one-half hours, while I napped in the chair or rigged baits near the transom. As we neared those clear blue-green waters of the stream, spreading in three directions like our blue frontier, he would shout above the engines, pointing to a greyhounding porpoise, a scattering of flying fish, or a lone man-of-war bird tracing the troughs like a cast boomerang. "Marvelous! Magnificent!" And he would sometimes beat his chest like an ape.

All through the fishing we worked as a team. He set out the outriggers; I prepared the rods and let back the baits. I wired the fish; he gaffed them. And sometimes, together, almost in the same breath, as the boat dipped and rocked past a weedline, we'd both sight a marlin or a rocketing wahoo, and, no matter how professional we pretended to be, we'd jump and yell and scream to the crew member dozing in the fighting chair. There was so much excitement then. We were sure we could do anything.

Now Dad watched from the helmseat as I brought down all the tackle—the light spinners, ice chest, and bait. Breathing heavily, he started the engine, squaring things away on the console. It was neither the same boat nor the same fishing now. We'd traded for a smaller, open craft that could only shuttle day trips through the estuaries and broad sounds to the barrier islands. Instead of marlin, now we hunted channel bass and black drum, which on light spinners could be almost as exciting. In the last two years, what we'd done was surf-fishing, and we had come to know it and accept it.

I stowed all the heavy gear, lugged some extra gas that Dad wanted on board, then jumped onto the dock, ready to cast off.

"The flag," he said, eyeing the bow.

"What?" I was anxious to get going now.

"The flag." He pointed to the naked rail mast, muttering, "To see the wind," and started rummaging through the gear, pulling things out onto the deck.

I shot a baffled expression at the back of his head, as if to say, "Do you really need to do all that for wind direction?" But he finally located it, then rose slowly, fumbling to find his bifocals, and sat on the bow rail to secure it with cumbersome monofilament. I could hear him breathing hard—a steamy sound through the nose—and I grew more impatient, as if I were waiting for a kettle to boil.

"You drive. Go where you think it's best." He motioned me to the helm and dropped into the closer and more comfortable passenger seat, looking, without expression, at the water. I remained on the dock, frozen, for quite a while. Then I jumped down, rubbed the wheel with the tips of my fingers. Backing quickly out of the slip, I turned the bow downriver and brought the boat to a plane.

Out on the open water, with the engine wailing and the awning flapping in the wind, it was too loud to talk. I wanted to say something, but couldn't. It was hard to begin. He had been so active, had done so much. How do you tell someone that he has to stop? Silently I began to search the sides of the river for signs of life, looking past his head, which rested on the windshield. It was low tide, and the slick mud banks of the river were fully exposed. The early afternoon sun, burdened with haze, blunted all color to a greasy gray. Quite soon I realized it was a time of day in which game would be sparse. Things were hiding in the marsh and the small hammocks and islands. The waters of the creeks were rippled with the tremors of our wake; large oyster rakes jutted from the shallows, menacing, hostile; a lone cormorant, perched on a snag, dried its wings in the lazy sun.

We rounded the bend where the river opened onto the sound, the spread of marsh disappointingly brown instead of the fanning green of summer. A stiff southeaster bellowed the awning against its frame, making the motion of the craft seem stiff on the chop. Chill spread on my skin like light water, and I began to think that it was going to be a disappointing afternoon. With a nervous frustration that seemed to increase with every wave we pounded, I began to long for those sultry June evenings of my past when we'd surf back from the stream with three hundred pounds of dolphin iced in the cooler, and a sailfish or marlin.

At the mouth of the sound the water looked like foamy root beer. I slowed and started to negotiate the breakers, which lapped around the bar I'd selected to fish. A flock of pelicans flushed slowly. Circling and splitting, they tipped their heads as if annoyed by our arrival, and left the bar as smooth and bare as the bald crown of an old man's head.

Dad tripped and banged his knee getting out of the boat. As he slopped in the ankle-deep water, trying to regain his balance, I found myself more aggravated than sympathetic.

"Take these rods." I was surprised at the tone of my order. But he took them without word or expression, and we trudged through the blue-hot sand, which squeaked under our feet, to the surf on the far side.

Attaching the pyramid sinker and leader to my line, I wondered what he was thinking. If only we can get him to slow down. He has to slow down. I watched him rig his rod deftly, then lace two huge prawns on the hooks and fill a small bait bucket with more.

"Good luck," he said as he turned and waddled into the breakers, stopping, flinching onto the tips of his toes with each wave to keep the white water from wetting his shirt.

Now I paid attention to my own fishing, wanting to concentrate on it and it alone, feeling that I was called upon now to catch something, to produce. I was using a different bait than he. Selecting the freshest mullet, I filleted a whole side and rigged my hook so the tail of meat could flap in the current—an unctuous, silver-blue flag to attract the passing fish. With the sharp knife, I quickly cut three more, picked a few shrimp from the bag, and headed for the water, a good fifty yards from my father.

I was looking for the vigorous surf of an outer bar, vibrant foam lapping on clear, green water. But the shallows were still turbid, and every time I approached a healthy set of waves they would fade, the white water looking like the dappled flank of a giraffe. The search took me quite a distance from my father. Finally, wading beyond a small slough, I found some breaking rollers and cast into them.

But even now that I was set, there seemed to be a continuing sense of unrest: a grating of frustrations, both internal and external, reflecting and feeding upon one another. It had seemed so much easier to fish back then, even when we went farther and were on more ocean. Back then, in the big boat, I seemed to ride the seemingly infinite energy of my father. But now I was by myself. The soothing layer of sun on my back began to be cut by the splash of roostertails crossing the surf. My meticulously prepared baits were beginning to disintegrate from the vexing nibbles of catfish. And as a final aggravation, the wing of a stingray grazed my ankle, causing me to flounder and hop, splash myself in the ridiculous dance of a coward, which I hoped my father hadn't noticed. I felt alone and powerless, there in the water. And somehow I began to blame all this on him.

The time came when I picked the last piece of bait from my bucket and laced the hook with it, washing my hands in the brine. Wading out as far as I could, I cast into the surf, then quickly retreated before the white water of a broken wave. Concentrating, I held the line with my index finger so I could feel the bite, then free-spool the line to some hungry bass. All energy, all focus were directed down that line, into the surf. And my back was still to my father.

Shark! I thought when it hit me. A cold, metallic fin seemed to brush my ankle, and as I turned and jumped, almost dropping my rod and falling, I saw my father standing a few feet behind me, laughing. His rod was unrigged and still in the water where my foot had been, and he began to cough, laughing. Then light tears came to his eyes, and they flushed clear. For a minute I stood, disbelieving, angry. He moved a step closer through the water, putting his hand on my shoulder, saying through the receding coughs and chuckles that made him squint, "Come on, let's go. Nothing but catfish here. I know where to go." It was a cold, wet, fisherman's hand at first, a hand that made me flinch, but then the warmth came through, and it was a father's hand which brought a smile to my face then a laugh out into the breeze, along with the sound of the surf.

"You old son of a bitch."

The flood tide pushed us from that barren bar. We decided that it wasn't really important to catch fish this evening. We had caught plenty of fish. With the turn of the current, the wind slackened, and the ebbing sea fell into series after series of docile swells. We rode across the beach-front of Osapa Island, taking the long way home, riding the waves like a giant white porpoise. There was a deer in the dunes, feeding on the spears of Spanish bayonets, and it never took its eyes off us as we passed. Snowy egrets dotted the seapines and wind-sculpted cedars like splatters of paint upon a green canvas.

We rounded the point into the sound, and the estuaries fanned into the marsh like the probing roots of some great tree. The sun glowed in its haze, its now-mellow light spreading over the water, accentuating the essence of the evening, the way that drawn butter and lemon brings out the taste of fresh crab. There was a pleasant commingling of suntan lotion and cut mullet in the air, and in the dunes a huge osprey nest rested in the fork of a dead oak. We had always talked about how we wished we would come back as those birds, living on the edge of the sea, being able to fall from sleep and into the languid flight of morning fishing.

Rocking gently into the smaller creeks, we began to pass huge rafts of dead marsh grass drifting slowly seaward. A lone heron rode one, standing on a single leg, shoulders hunched, looking like a gentleman in a gray flannel coat. And now as I drove, turning into the first sweep of the narrows, it was as if our motion had caught up with the movement of time and was carefully synchronizing with it. I could feel my father standing beside me, and he knew too. There was no need to talk now, and I eased down on the throttle, the wind across my face pulling water from my eyes.

THE WAY IT WAS BEFORE

THINGS GOT NEW

Art Lee sat and looked at the three men slumped under the slash pine hedgerow. One of them picked at his teeth with a whittled camphor twig while the other two would drop off to sleep, unknowingly nod their heads forward, then jerk up in bewilderment.

They were all older than Art. He figured it was this condition that now caused them to be so stifled by the midday heat. He could understand their lethargy, too.

The cycle of afternoon rain, humid air rising sunward from the moist earth, and dull thunderheads building by dinner seemed almost permanent. In this weather the packhouse was rough even for a man as young and solid as Art. More than once he had faltered in that building, the heavy mixture of tobacco tars and sugars, heat and steam almost suffocating him.

Scratching his hair, he rose slowly. He still used a dab of bacon grease to condition the wiry strands, even though there was a wide array of sweet-smelling conditioners and latest "hair kits" on the market. There was no real reason in his doing this. It was only something he'd done ever since he was old enough to heed instruction from his mother, who, in turn, had used the bacon grease because it was the only affordable and, most of all, attainable substance. His face, unlike the three other men—and, for that matter, any other black man in Odum, Georgia —had grizzled whiskers that coated his wide jaw, then blended into his hairline above the ear. At a distance the beard was indiscernible. The man's skin was as black as tar paper, and his eyes, sinking back into his thick skull, looked like melting pieces of hail. Still gazing at the three men, he took it upon himself to end the already extended lunch break.

"I do believe it's going to rain this evening," he said,

eyeing the high clouds in the west. "So I imagine we'd better get the 'bacca on that truck so he can get it to market when he gets back."

The men rose reluctantly, as if some type of judgment might take place within the cypress-board walls of the house. The sheets usually felt heavier on this first load of the year.

"He's right." Cliff took the pick out of his teeth and sucked on the end. "That 'bacca ain't going to walk on that truck by itself."

The four men ambled to the house. Art and Cliff stood on the bed of the tandem-wheeled truck parked at the door, while Larry and Charlie disappeared into the darkness and grabbed a sheet. They returned, shuffling crablike over the burlap mass, and swung it onto the steel body of the truck.

"How you going to fit all these sheets on this truck, Art?" Larry shuffled back out of the light with Charlie.

"Five high and cap with one, I reckon," he said. He had worked as a top loader for a number of years, and by the end of a summer he could pack one hundred and fifty sheets onto the big company semis that would haul the crop to the factories in North Carolina and Virginia.

"There was a time when it would take a whole season to have fifty sheets a 'bacca," Larry said as he and Charlie returned and heaved the second. "Mr. Randall would take only eight sheets at a time to market, and we'd hand pack every one a the things and load them on the back of his pickup like they was made a gold." They brought another.

"That 'bacca back then looked like gold." Cliff caught a sheet and moved with Art to the front of the truck. "I don't think there wasn't one handful of it that didn't go top dollar. That frog-eyed–looking stuff would have all a them buyers throwing their hands up come auction time."

"That was a good time." Larry slung another sheet. "Back then when we'd stay a whole day at the market."

"Yeah, you talking," Cliff said.

"I'd be sipping that smooth whiskey with one hand and trying to keep my Willy down what's seeing all them fine, whorey-looking womens with the other," Larry said. "It was like a country fair or something; seemed like everybody was celebrating."

They all stopped and stood by the door with chests heaving slightly and sweat beading on their sepia bodies. Art Lee took off his shirt, exposing his wide chest, arms looking like smoothly crafted, blued steel. He glanced at the white farmhouse shaded by a cluster of pecan trees, and noticed the two white children making their way across the flat lawn towards the packhouse. Their course was unsteady. Every so often they spurted into a choppy run that would lose itself. Keenly, slowly, they would examine a small tree or piece of farm machinery, only to revive and chase a chicken or a rooster. By the time the black men started throwing the sheets again, young Randy and Bill were in the packhouse with them.

The two romped about the tobacco sheets and screamed, running from the "tobacco monster," which they had been told by Larry lived in the rafters of the ancient warehouse. "You boys better not go around up high on them sheets. That 'bacca monster gonna come down on you from his ceiling top."

Their playing slowed the men's work, but they were tolerated. Charlie and Larry even allowed them to ride on the sheets from the dark and musty corners of the building to the doorway. There the boys would jump down to the ground, sprint, chattering and giggling, between the steel bed of the truck and the cracked boards of the house to the back door, and climb back in just as the men were picking up another sheet. They made a game of it. Soon, though, the children were as weary as the men, and they complained of thirst, even though their pale skin was only flushed with a slight film of sweat.

"Why don't you boys go get us all some water from the house?" Cliff's nostrils flared as he breathed and pulled out a yellowed handkerchief. The young boys looked at the four men, black, standing at the doorway with the sun still drawing liquid from their bodies.

"Will you ride us on the sheets some more when we get back?" Bill asked.

"Sure, young'un," Charlie said. "We'll find the biggest sheet to set you on."

"OK," the boys said and started towards the house.

"Bring some ice in it," Larry shouted at them.

The men sat on the back of the truck, waiting, absorbing the sporadic breaths of wind while Art walked over to the spigot. He swallowed the warm water, then dipped his shirt under the stream and wiped his long muscles.

In the west, clouds were beginning to mount, billowing in confused shades of gray and white with the sun arcing downwards, seeming to coax them into its set course. A group of katydids blurted. Bill and Randy trooped back, heavy with the water and the cups that had been dropped three times in coming. By now, the men's blood was pulsing through their bodies more slowly and evenly, and their breathing subsided into a smooth set of rhythms. Giving the water to Cliff, the boys climbed to the doorway and sat among the hands.

"Let me have some," Randy said.

Cliff poured two cups for the children, and they took a few gulps, then just held the cups. Larry and Charlie downed three, and Cliff had two, and Art had already drunk the warm spigot water, so he sat with twin veins mapping a ridge down his biceps. Randy stood, sloshing some water on Larry, who looked up and grinned.

"Art Lee," Randy said. "Ride me on that big 'bacca sheet."

"We done moved all the big sheets, Randy," he said. "You gonna have to wait till we take another load."

"But I want to ride."

"We gonna have work to do in a minute now. You can wait, can't you?"

"No," Randy said. "I want to ride."

"Why don't you ride the boy, Art?" Larry swallowed the water.

"Yeah, ride us," Bill said.

"We ain't got time," he said. "We got to finish this water and get the rest a the 'bacca on the truck. Look at that storm cloud coming. You boys ought to go home now."

Randy pulled a mouthful from his cup, puffing out his checks. Looking straight at Art's ebony face, he spit the water on his head.

His eyes cut up at the child, seeming to rise out of the heavy skull in which they were bedded. "Don't do that again, boy. People don't spit water on people like that."

Randy grinned, pulled from his cup, filled his mouth, and sprayed him again.

"That chile got a will of his own," Larry chuckled.

With his eyes still fixed on the boy, Art reached up and slapped him solidly on the shoulder, catching the side of his puffy face and batting the cup to the floor. At first Randy did nothing, then his face widened, tears welled and came out in a long, intensifying whine.

"You shouldn't a hit that boy," Cliff said.

Randy broke into a pathetic bellow; his brother slunk away from Art, eyes widening. Then, like a flushed pair of quail, the two ran off to an adjacent stick barn that now served as an equipment shed.

"What did you do that for?" Larry said.

"I told him not to spit." He looked at all of them. "I warned him. You don't let young'uns do that. They're not supposed to go around spitting on everyone."

"He's gonna be mad when he finds this out," Charlie said. "That ain't none a our business."

The men crumpled their cups and set the cooler aside. Larry and Charlie scuffed back into the darkness and started throwing the sheets. Not really having dried off from their break, the same sweat came again. Art stacked the tobacco. He wasn't looking at the three older men now, but occasionally he'd catch sight of the two white children who were playing in the sand under the barn.

He remembered when he was a youngster, the way it was before things got new. It was when he'd walk behind the croppers and pick up the ripe tobacco leaves dropped on the ground, then carry an armload over to the sled. He'd do it all summer, with the hot sun overhead and the hot sand on his feet. He remembered how much water he'd drink back then, drinking from the galvanized cooler even when his belly was so full that it ballooned over his belt.

Then when the sun was full in the pale sky he'd feel it in his head and, falling behind the others, lie down in the scant shade of the plants, digging what Mr. Randall called "gopher holes" whenever he caught him. Then he'd always get up and catch up, even though he still felt the sun in his head and the bloat of water in his stomach, the hot heat up above, the burning sand around his feet.

The market was something that came only four times a summer, and he looked forward to it. Mr. Randall would drive to the house and get him with the eight sheets packed neatly on the bed of the truck. He would get back there on the tobacco, and Mr. Randall would say, "Watch out for them sheets for me now, son. We wouldn't want none of them to fall out on the highway, would we now? We'd have a real mess then, for sure." And he would return, "Yessah," looking at the cab of the pickup with Mr. Randall's furrowed neck and dusty gray hat showing and a small white boy's face peering back through the thick glass. They were the only two in the front, and he was the only one on the tobacco. All of the long drive to Blackshear, he could smell the tobacco along with the rusty odor of the burlap sheets, and the wind would make his nose feel flat, scraping tears from his eyes. He'd always see Mr. W.D.'s pigs wallowing in the same mud hole every time he'd go, and he remembered how he laughed at the pigs, thinking to himself that as long as they lived, those sorry-looking fathead pigs would never be able to get out of their mud hole, and never really want to, either.

Then they'd dip into the swamp bottom, and he remembered how Mr. Randall would hang his head out of the window and tell him to look for "venisons," as he put it. But he never really looked. His eyes might have scanned the thick fringe of cypress and water oaks that tightly pressed the highway's straight course, but he just felt the wind on his face and would sometimes think about the taste of the deer meat that Mr. Randall would bring over to his house in the winter.

For some reason it would always be warmer when they'd bank out of the swamp and be where the houses had sidewalks and the streets had lights. He remembered that he became uneasy in the back of the truck by himself, riding through the city. It was after he'd heard from his uncle Jimmy that one of his cousins had been shot in

Blackshear, and that people got shot almost every week in Blackshear. From that time on, when he was little, he nestled behind the cab of the truck, scanning the storefronts and alleys for people that he thought might have a gun. He wished he could have been in the cab of the truck with Mr. Randall and his son, Billy. He didn't like being both scared and alone.

When they'd pull into the large Planter's Warehouse, under the elaborate shelter of heart pine trusses and beams, and Mr. Randall and Billy would get out of the truck, he would forget about getting shot and hop off the bed. While Mr. Randall weighed in the tobacco, he and Billy would play among the open sheets that lined the floor and smelled like cane syrup or, at least, something sweet and edible.

The two would race in and out of the piles, go to the far, dark corners of the building, and lie on the sheets when they were too winded to run anymore. Mr. Randall would always call them after he'd tended to his business and had talked with some of the other farmers. When they got back, he'd have two large orange sodas for them, and he would drink his fast, looking up at the white men grouped around chewing and spitting tobacco on the floor that had been wearied from the thousands of sheets, the thousands of dirt farmers that had scuffed its wide boards. When the talk had mellowed and the sun was dipping westward, they'd get in the truck and make the trip back.

He never really felt too good going back to Odum. The sheets of tobacco were gone and the steel that he sat on was hard, and he could never find a comfortable place to rest his head. His stomach always felt tight because he'd drunk the cold drink too fast; the taste of orange usually soured about halfway back. He would start to doze, but the truck would jar over the pits in the road, banging his head against the hard metal.

"Eddie's about the only one who'll make shine won't make your head feel like it's going to explode off," Larry said, and his voice pulled him from his thoughts. "These days you got to watch your man. Sell you some white liquor that'll either taste weak like rain water or rank like diesel fuel."

Another sheet hit the truck. He stacked it with Cliff.

"Ol' Eddie right reasonable." Cliff strained. "That brown liquor will put a good head on you. Put a peppermint stick in the bottom of a jug, and it won't taste half bad, either."

"Sure enough," Charlie smiled.

"I saw ol Pee-Wee on Sunday, when he got hold to a jug a it," Cliff said. "He's walking around like he been shot at and missed, shit at and hit. His eyes were all bugged out like a boiled owl. And you could smell him a mile down the road."

"He musta drunk the whole jug." Charlie threw a sheet.

"And you should a seen Janey getting after him," Cliff said.

"That right?"

"Man, she hollered him down and told him he was nothing but a hog in a waller. And she was never going to feed him again and she was never going to let him in the house and that he might as well find some other place."

A feeble breeze circled the door of the packhouse as the fiftieth sheet slapped the bed of the truck. Sweating, they stood wiping the fluids from their faces and talking about good liquor and bad. He had quit listening. Billy would be back soon, he thought. Watching the clouds in the west, he remained planted, thinking that at least it would be cool when the rains came, then remembering that more water would mean the tobacco patch would be boggier. There was a time when they had cropped on foot, and the showers were always welcome. Shade and water cooled the workers. Now the soft soil would only pull a machine down and stop the whole operation. With Billy's sixty-acre allotment, as opposed to Mr. Randall's six, there was no time to waste, for water at this time of year only rusted metal and broke axles. Once the leaves hued to a pale gold, they would have to be harvested, packed into the shiny bulk barns, pressure cooked, crammed into the sheets, and hauled to the market.

He liked to work on the new pickers and load the tobacco fast, even if the pace was demanding. This was no excuse to handle the crop sloppily, though, and he concentrated on caring for every process the leaves went through. It gave him the same feeling he would sometimes have when he and Billy were the running backs for Glenn County High and carried their team to the state playoffs —the physical work; the quickness; the courage to run head-on into the defensive line; the ability to make it across the goal; and the sweat that came afterwards, not rank or useless, but the product of a test and a victory.

Low, resonant thunder was rolling from the blue line of clouds that closed in from the west. The tree line across the fields took on a silver cast, for the wind was in it, bending the tops so that the undersides of the leaves were bared and swaying as if they were surrendering to the weather before it arrived.

"O mercy!" Charlie looked straight at him.

The two white children raced towards their father as a tan pickup rattled towards the packhouse, throwing up a trail of dust that was sucked eastward into the only patch of clear sky. The temperature had dropped. The wind whipped, rattling through the corn and raising small eddies of dirt around the door. Billy pulled beside the big truck, jumped out, and looked at Art. "Y'all got all the 'bacca loaded?"

"It's on the truck," he said.

"Daddy." Bill ran towards his father. "Art slapped Randy and made him cry."

"What, son?"

"Art Lee slapped me and wouldn't ride me on the big 'bacca sheet." Randy renewed his sobs.

"It's going to storm," he said to the children. "You better go home to your mother before you get wet."

The boys jumped down and ran, looking back at the packhouse, stumbling, then eyeing the billowing storm behind it.

"What happened out here?" Billy looked at Art, who stood solidly in front of him. The three older men sort of shielded their eyes in the doorway of the packhouse.

"Randy spit water on me," he said, his eyes glued to the white man who stood as a physical equal. "He did it once and I warned him. He did it again, and I slapped him."

The smell of rain was now in the gusting wind, coming from the west, the heart of the storm, then across and around the dormant stick barns, the metallic bulk barns, to the truck and eastward.

"He spit on you?" Billy said. "I've told you all to keep those children in line if they get to doing things like that. If they get to bothering you while you work, send them home." He looked at the clouds coming. "Art, come on with me. It'll give us the ride to Blackshear to plan how we're going to rotate these barns out. Let's get the tarp and make market before this stuff gets wet. The rest of you knock off for the evening. We're going to pick in the morning. I'll be around at six."

"Yessah," they said, all three in the door of the packhouse with the darkness behind them, the thick smell of rancid sweat and tobacco pushed in around them by the gusts of the oncoming storm.

He and Billy got in the cab of the ten-wheeled truck together. Billy turned the engine over and headed down the road. They stopped at the barn and secured a red tarp over the bundles in back, then pulled onto the highway, south, to Blackshear, winding through the gears and picking up speed slowly. The storm was swinging north and east, and out in front of the fast-moving clouds, thunder cracked and rolled like invisible foam in front of a broken wave.

RETRIEVING

It would have been a time for talk: a time for full-lunged speculation, even jokes to best the wind and the cold. But we were silent, and for a while I couldn't bring myself to look at him.

The northwester had been blowing all night. Blasts of frigid air rolled over the tidewater flatland like the white water of some massive wave, and as we hit the open water, progress began to seem low, pitiful. From time to time, regripping the bow cord for support, I tried to imagine the place as I had known it so many times, in the serenity of a summer's breeze. But this quickly proved useless. There were only cold and distant silhouettes bending painfully against the star-punctured sky.

The three of us—two young men and a dog—hunched in the aluminum duck boat, and even the animal, Bull William, a seal-like Labrador retriever, lay quivering in the bottom of the skiff as the water began to slap the bow and shower in a needling mist. My friend Jasper guided the three-horse Evinrude, pitch varying as we hit the chop. Facing the weather, I broke the spray and was glad that we'd already put on our waders at the landing. Inwardly I was riddled too, confused by the talk that occurred during the long drive from the city. Recalling it made me want to hunch down like the dog and let the frigid spray cut into my companion.

Had he changed so? My head swarmed with depressing images of what he had said.

Before I went off to college, I had never questioned our friendship. (This was my first year at a small college in Boston.) Hell, Jasper and I had grown up together, had hunted together during high school years, had excitedly tested ourselves on those first hunts where we were permitted to venture forth alone. We had worked hard with the dogs in the summers; we had scouted for places to hunt on those autumn afternoons; we had dreamt of the perfect hunt; we had been let down in the cold, had topped our waders in bogs of chill water.

But the first thing I noticed when he picked me up this morning was a harsh twang to his accent. Maybe it had always been there? But now it seemed to challenge me.

In his large Buick Estate Wagon we had driven from the residential section, passing the large gray-brick and stucco houses. They were set between stable oaks and huge magnolias that were probably older than the city itself; and the orange tint of the corner lights, the mere size and stability of these houses against the wind, the buzz of the car's heater, gave an aura of great security. We both had grown up there. We felt comfortable there.

At first there were the greetings, the normal excited talk and speculation amidst the nosings and exuberant licks of the dog.

"Yeah, they some teal and woodies around." Jasper spewed the words in a blast of cigarette smoke. "Them big ducks, them mallards and blacks, most a them been stopped by them bastards baiting up on the Chesapeake."

"I'd be satisfied with a limit on woodies," I said. "They eat better than any of them."

He had nodded, making a strange, almost nervous,

seething sound. I figured he was worried about the out-
come of the hunt.

No longer having to slow for lights and turns, I was
relieved that we traveled quickly and that there were no
street lamps in the outskirts. We started to pass the decaying frame dwellings of Yamacraw Village. Every time I
would go through that battered settlement without the
silent shield of darkness, it always seemed ashen gray and
junk-piled with people, black people crammed and stifled
by the surroundings. It was like passing through a threat-
ening, dark corridor. It always did something to me, too,
made me feel wrong about living sometimes; especially in
the massive town house I'd grown up in.

And just as I was thinking about all this, Jasper had
come out with it, his voice sounding alien as if he were
some kind of anachronistic creature.

"Those were the days," he said, resting his hand on the
black dog beside him. "I wish I'd lived back then." From
our heated bubble, he looked out at the houses we passed.
Again there was the seething sound as he blew out the
cigarette smoke.

"What are you talking about?" At first I thought I'd
missed something in my reverie.

"You mean your Daddy never had a Yamacraw retriever?"

"A what?"

"Yamacraw retriever. Full-bred, bull nigger, without papers, unfortunately. Shit, every dove hunt Dad would go on he'd visit the village first. If he could have figured out a way to get them to swim, he probably would have gotten a Yamacraw for ducks, too. They're awfully good at pouring coffee."

Still a bit confused, I blurted a terse chuckle.

"I went with him once when I first got my .410. All he'd have to do was to find a checker game of old darkies or a group of young'uns playing ball, and the rest was easy pickings. He'd ride up real slow, roll down the window, and hang a five-dollar bill out, saying, 'which one a you wants to pick up some birds for me this evening?' Sometimes he could even do it with a $3.45 pint bottle of vodka. And they'd be jumping at the car like a bunch of hounds at a gut bucket."

I could not read my friend as he said all this. There was still the nervous, constricted seething in his voice, as if he were reacting to something rather than relating an experience. I could see his eyes switching nervously from battered dwelling to battered dwelling and then to me as we sped through Yamacraw. At that point I began to fidget and perspire.

The heater, his voice, the constant smoke, seemed to taint his whole being, as if some highly corrosive element had spilled onto him. The volition to do something drastic—to grab him and shake him, to merely get out of the car—wormed through my insides. But then, strange, as we started to get out into the country and pass small fields, the first bottom, then creeks, I began to notice that Jasper was relaxing. He started to talk pleasantly about his last hunt.

When at last we had started on the river, sitting in the cold, feeling those first brutal blasts of wind, the frustrations came again. I began to be angry and then my wrath drained into a feeling of numbness and depression. It was as if some whole part of my life were getting plummeted, torn away.

How was it? Here was my friend, someone I'd grown up with, someone I knew as well as anybody. Methodically I began to search our past for hints of something wrong. Hunching down in the cold spray I started to recall an instance where we couldn't have been more than seven or eight, right before we got our first shotguns.

We were at his house on the river one Saturday in late winter. During that time, we would rise early in the morning, grab our BB guns and be off—exploring the acres of mature forest which lined the river bluff.

It was after lunch, because it was only the call of our stomachs that could bring us near the house. I remembered their yardman, Efram, driving up in his old Buick, the tools of his trade—rakes, hoes, shovels, a wheelbarrow and lawnmower—jutting from the back windows and open trunk which flapped obliviously and banged lazily. He drove up the long oyster shell drive no faster than a walk. Even at that young age, I could sense something tragic—the same disjunct, brutal essence of poverty that emanated from Yamacraw. I wondered if Jasper and his father had sensed it, too.

As the car neared the house, Blitz, Jasper's father's enormous Labrador, started to bark explosively, circling and charging, nipping at the tires and fenders of the slowly moving car. We were all standing at the back of the house with Jasper's father, who was showing us how to hit pinecones on the low branches. Then all of that stopped and we were watching the car and could see Efram and his son, about our age, frantically rolling up the windows. Jasper's father sort of moved in front of us, crossing his arms, a small slant of a smile on the corner of his face.

Finally, after they'd stopped, Efram rolled down the window just a crack. Jutting, twisting his huge mouth up towards the tiny space, he called timidly, "I'se here, Mr. Jasper, we all here now."

As if annoyed, Jasper's father called the dog off, slowly,

seeming to relish its final nips at the dilapidated sedan. Then Efram got out.

Jasper's father started to walk Efram around the house and lawns, pointing out work with a stick. After quite some time Efram's son, Rabbit, slunk out of the car. He had very long arms and his forehead slanted back to his hairline, making his eyes seem especially large, sad. Looking around him, he was still a bit jumpy, but his curiosity over our hunting clothes and BB guns started to overpower the fear.

We were still shooting at a few pinecones. Rabbit moved closer. We started to fill the magazines with BB's, ready to strike out for the woods. Out of the blue Jasper had looked at him and said, "You want to come with us?"

Rabbit had nodded, scuffing at the ground with his sneaker.

"We'll find you a big stick and make it into a gun for you."

You could see Rabbit's confidence coming into his eyes. He jumped forward, sprinting, and we all started to run for the woods.

Just as we started to climb the hog wire fence that surrounded the kept grounds, Jasper's father and Efram rounded the corner of the house.

"Where are you three going?" Jasper's father's voice boomed and stopped us.

"After squirrels and catbirds in the back woods," Jasper said, squinting hopefully.

"Well," his father said. "You only got two guns." There was a tightness in his voice as he walked up. Efram was trailing, lumbering.

"That's all right," Jasper had said. "We're going to make him a gun out of a stick."

"He can share mine, sometimes," I had said meekly.

Then Jasper's father started walking in a circle. He looked frantically around the house, a steamy kind of breathing coming from his nose, his eyes switching.

"Wait," he said, his eyes resting on the backlawn. "I'm gonna need Rabbit this afternoon. He has to work. See all those pinecones on the lawn? I want them picked up. You want to make a quarter this afternoon, don't you, son?"

I could see the wetness pushing into the corner of Rabbit's large eyes. He shrunk into himself and crept towards the two big men.

"Hurry up over here," Efram said, "fore I take a stick to you." When Rabbit got to him, Efram grabbed his ear and twisted it.

Jasper and I had slowly climbed the fence and entered the woods. We stopped and looked at Rabbit as he stooped to pick up the cones we had been shooting down. We could still hear him crying. I had looked over at Jasper.

There was a look of pure horror in his eye. It looked as if he might cry any second. He turned and saw me looking, then turned away.

Low, in the rustle of the leaves, still in sight of the house and grounds, scraping then seething, I had heard Jasper whisper "nigger," using the word as if he were constructing a shield around himself.

Now I tried to shiver my feeling of horror away. The icy water was beginning to soak through my parka at the collar. The stars in the sky were almost throbbing, and in front of the lights of the city I could see the billowing, low shapes of the hammocks in the marsh. "But it's such goddamn beautiful country." I almost yelled it into the cold.

My job now was to look for a series of breaks in the bank, ancient rice canals, built years ago by slaves, that would allow us to broach the wind, slip towards the direction where the sun would rise, and do it all with the tall black mud banks, the swaying reeds, and marsh grass sheltering us in the slack tide. I noticed micalike crusts of ice forming on my waders and was all the more eager to get out of the big river.

Abruptly, as the boat caught a whitecap on the bow, the decoys clanking against the side and the dog's paws grating over the aluminum, I caught sight of the first narrow slit and pointed. "There we go," was all I said, and the boat veered into the canal mouth, final waves clapping the gunwale, torque of the engine rising, seeming to wail our relief now that we were no longer headed by the chop. Here, there were only the ripples raking the flat bottom of the boat in a subsiding set of rhythms, and I felt hints of the first calm of the morning.

I looked at the avenue of slick water, reeds swaying, the wind almost blowing them flat. The chill now barely brushed the top of my head. The canal, silver, almost paved-looking, narrowed somewhat, and on the edge, jutting from the mud, were the occasional cedar stumps and snags that had been cut when the canal was trenched.

Then we talked, and Bull William was up in the well between the two low seats, sitting rigidly, head pointed back towards Jasper, who now sucked casually on a cigarette and said, "That there ain't good for nobody."

"Good wind, though."

"Only for ducks." He slung his hand over the dog's neck, and you could hear the tail start to rap wildly on the metal. "He's got enough hide on him, though. He'll be swimming this morning."

"I damn sure ain't going sloshing in after any birds." I laughed, finally glad it was this kind of talk and no more silence. "At least I hope I won't have to."

"Don't worry," Jasper smiled, "Ol' Bull baby, ol' tar-headed nigra baby here done growed up enough to do it right. You might even be surprised."

Come on, Jasper, I said to myself, not out here and hunting. But that was all I could do; say it to myself and try to look beyond it. Still looking through the alley of bending grasses, I could see the faint glow of Savannah off east. At least there was a distance out here and we were doing something.

My thoughts calmed again, shifting to the summer and the river, always the river with Jasper and Bull William on the dock with the dummy. Then, I had sensed something interesting, almost beautiful between the man and the beast.

The dog would be planted at his master's foot, tail sweeping the wooden planks, and Jasper would throw the dummy into the river with the dog not moving, all movement inside: the gathering and bulking of muscles. Then Jasper would stand back, and Bull would look up at him, then at the dummy bobbing and drifting slowly off the ebb tide, and the dog would remain. Jasper would say, "Hack," and Bull's head would push forward, body painfully stationary. "Sack," and again, only the eager eyes would dart. Finally, in no more than a whisper, he'd utter the proper command, "Back," and all the compressed muscle and sinew would explode, the dog in flight, stretching and paddling, crashing into the water towards the buoy. Then Jasper would take the biscuit from his pocket, look calmly over to me, and say, "He's just a young'un. Gotta teach him something about phonetics every now and then." And we would laugh as the dog stroked back against the current.

Bull William's all right, I thought, full ready to see the animal go after a duck, knowing that Jasper had, indeed, done well, and that he could train a dog with a precision yet not sap the personality, the buoyance from the animal in doing so. It was such a wonderfully simple and easy relationship between Jasper and his dog. It was all right for a man and dog to be bound together like that. I looked back and said, "I won't believe a thing Bull does until I see it."

"Just wait." Jasper nodded, beading eyes and thin nose beaming from under his floppy hat. "But you gonna have to hit them birds before he does his work."

The passage banked slightly to the right, avoiding a low hammock of myrtles, then branched and opened into a fork.

"Get them decoys." Jasper slowed the engine. I grabbed the sack and started pulling the magnum mallard hens and drakes out, unraveling the weights and cords. The boat passed the point, circling and turning, while one by one I tossed the leaden sinkers, decoys following, smacking the water. Then the small flock of ten were in random grouping, colorless, moving already against the constant wind.

Jasper steered to the opposite point, killed the engine, and with only the gusts rippling the high grass we drifted to the bank. As soon as the bow nudged the mud Bull was out. Clanking and fumbling, we moved the gear, the guns, and shells, transferred heavy camouflage parkas and thermoses to a large plyboard already set in the marsh. Finally Jasper pulled the motor up, got out, and we both hoisted the light craft up the sharp embankment and into the reeds. All smooth, we worked silently now, moving as freely as well-oiled gears meshing together. And the dog crackled at our heels, sloshing the mud, tail slinging water, excitedly surveying the final camouflaging of the boat as we broke reeds and tented saw palms over the engine.

It was still good dark by the time we reached the board which overlooked the decoys from the point. We sorted through the shells, loading the heavy twelve-gauge automatics with high brass duck loads. Prepared, I poured two coffees from a thermos and drank. Bull plopped onto the plank at Jasper's foot, and before he took the coffee he gave the dog some water from a little jug. We faced the wind, felt it as it curled the steam from the cups, drafting the heat from the coffee. I was ready now, cradling the mug, gripping my Browning in the free hand, and drawing the coffee which I'd spiked slightly with brandy.

Then he hissed, "Yessir," quickly crouching and placing his cup on the board. I followed mechanically, the whistling of wings so quick it was like an auditory mirage grazing my head. I turned, facing the east, and with the northwester, it looked as if the whole tidal system — the reeds, the marsh, the flagging cattails, the dwarfed hammock trees — was all bowing that way, genuflecting the oncoming light in smooth sibilance. The sun creased the horizon and with it came the ducks, beating black silhouettes at first, winging and circling in tight groups of eights and tens. All across the sky now blazing with color, distant strands of birds trailed like fine black threads.

Heads down, we now fingered our guns, eyes stretching out from under the rims of hats. Jasper grabbed the call in his free hand and blew. I could see the whites of his eyes cornering, moving almost in conjunction with the choppy cackle of the feeding call. Out in front the decoys, caught by the gusts, swam against their nylon cords, pivoting in tight circles, animated movement.

Against the wind, a flight of mallards pitched in, webbed feet flaring, reaching for the water, rocking and streaming. We beaded up and fired, orange blasts belching as shells ejected. The ducks, three of them, tumbled into the calm around the decoys. Jasper bent forward and, with a sweep of the arm, said, "Back." The dog was through the water with a power of maturity I hadn't noticed during the summer. Bull's head was pushing forward, nostrils open, and underneath the webbed feet, all four of them, were grabbing at the icy water. I could see that as the shoulder blades worked against each other.

"He'll double up," Jasper said. He focused on Bull as the dog moved, pulled closer to the ducks that had fallen and drifted, only two backs bobbing, closer together. Bull neared, mouth opening; and arching his neck out of the water, he grabbed the nearest duck. The dog started to turn but then saw the other bird slighted by the wind and heard Jasper and set a new course. I could see the confusion that Bull felt as he came upon the second mallard, his mouth already crammed with the first. It made him momentarily tread water, but then he was on the other bird, and Jasper was calling him, coaxing and coaching. After several passes, fondling and nudging the two, Bull managed to clamp lightly on both necks, and when he turned, the carcasses framing his wide head, he quickened his stroke, huffing and sneezing.

By the time the dog reached the bank, Jasper's face

was lit up. "Goddamn, unbelievable!" he said. Like a child he could hardly contain his excitement, and almost jumped as Bull sloshed up.

We began to have to work for the ducks, which is almost always the rule after the initial dawn flurry fades and the light distills. Jasper was in his element, totally relaxed, confident. His quick eye would catch a small thready V of mallards working against the wind and he would hunch down with the call, bellowing the three-cycle hailing call, causing the birds to shift cautiously, wheel in whip-the-rope fashion, then circle above.

He'd then break into the low clucking of the feeding call punctuated with an intermittent "wack," and the big ducks would start to set their winds. Finally, after minutes of having to watch the mallards circle tediously, we'd see them drop and sweep into the decoys and we'd shoot. And then Bull William would spring into action.

Within an hour we had our limits. We poured some more coffee, the cold now beginning to seep back around us as the shooting and retrieving and excitement subsided. It was a good achey feeling now with eight ducks at our feet and the bright tidal plain bonding out to the horizon.

Bull William wagged around Jasper's feet, and he played with the dog, saying "mallards" and then watching Bull crouch down and intently scan the sky for more birds.

"He's a good 'un, ain't he?"

"Sure is," I said. "You trained him better than any Lab I know."

"Ain't no Yamacraw retriever could do that, could they?" Jasper blurted. "You couldn't even get them out from around those gas heaters on a morning like this."

"I'm ready to go now," I said.

"All right," he said. "Ain't much more we can do here anyway but get cold."

We saw one flight of teal skitter across the marsh as we neared the mouth of the canal, guns oiled and in their cases, decoys bagged, engine droning behind Jasper. Now in full daylight, the water of the big river was speckled with the whitecapped chop—the silver-blue, brackish flow.

Slightly upriver, low against the far marsh, a small boat seemed to be bobbing helplessly.

"What's that?" Jasper slowed the engine a bit, squinting.

"I don't know, probably some fool trying to catch a fish."

"Don't think too many fishing fools would be out in this blow. That boat looks dead in the water and I don't see anybody in it." Jasper headed the boat into the waves, towards the small, bobbing craft. The cold water once again showered over us, and I braced against it, annoyed at having to go upriver. I was hungry and ready to get away from Jasper. I was tired and confused by what he said and what I had remembered. I was cold, too, very cold.

As we neared the boat, we could see the back of a person huddled between the seats, kind of rocking and jerking at the same time. An ancient Johnson motor, which recently had been repainted by brush, was pulled up and I could see a tangle of heavy wire around the prop. The pin was most likely sheared. There were some large catfish almost frozen in the bow of the boat, along with some trot lines wrapped around Clorox jugs.

Suddenly the person, hearing our motor, popped up. He turned towards us, waving his hands spastically. He was a young black man in a thin army jacket and blue skullcap.

At once, I looked back at Jasper, whose face was raw and red and whose camouflage parka was soaked and now thin-looking, so thin you could almost see through it. His countenance had not changed. He said nothing, just guided the boat steadily.

"Get a rope ready," he ordered, a very serious but relaxed look on his face. We came alongside, and I grabbed the side of the small boat, wondering what Jasper would do.

"What's the trouble?" he said. "Lost a pin?"

"Ran over sumpin' up creek. Tore up my engine. Ain't

got no pliers. Couldn't use 'em eben if I had 'em." The man could barely talk, he was so cold. He held up his gloveless hands like they were dead sticks.

"You running trot lines up in the fresh water?"

"Yep," the man said, moving slowly to the seat.

"Where did you put in? Up at Polk's?"

The man nodded.

Bull William had risen from his nest in between the sacks of decoys and was quietly eyeing the man and the boat.

"Can we pull you down to Turner's?" Jasper said. "I'd rather not try to go upriver towing a boat, even though it's not that far."

"Sho' would appreciate it. Anything to get me out a this cold. I can call my father-in-law to come on down and get me. He can fix engines."

"Come on and get on in with us," Jasper said, offering his hand.

As the man tried to get in, boats bobbing and clanking sloppily together, the dog laid its ears back and suddenly started barking, snapping.

"You!" Jasper grabbed the animal by the ear and gave it a sharp twist. "Get back down in your place."

Bull William, confused, still huffing and now eyeing both of them, came to the bow with me.

"He won't hurt you. He's too tired from retrieving. I think he thinks you might be coming to get his ducks." Jasper got the man over the gunwale. "Bull's always in a bad mood after a hunt until we can warm him up and give him some breakfast."

The black man sort of grunted, trying to smile.

"Why don't you pour the man some hot coffee?" Jasper barked at me, seemingly annoyed at my just sitting there.

"Sure," I said.

"And hand back that bow line so I can tie him off."

I couldn't help grinning as I handed the man the coffee. I was sure he would appreciate the bit of brandy in it. I looked at Jasper. The thought of him being a retriever almost made me laugh.

We could head downriver with the wind at our backs. The waves were moving with us, and I could feel the purity of the air heavy on this river.

Now I could conjure the summer. I knew the system of estuaries well then, had summered in their sultry afternoons as had Jasper. In my mind I traced the course of the tributary all the way down to the sound and the golden isles that flanked it, lulled and pulled by the ebb. I thought of the black mud and ooze and its powerful aroma of life and death, the snowy egrets as they fished in the flats and shallows, the soupy water mixing with the brine at the sounds and the people who harvested the crops of the marsh — all kinds of people — black crabbers, wealthy tournament fishers, lazy sailors — all at ease and working or not working in the summer's rhythms of these waters. Every August evening, soft, easterly breezes blew thunderheads up the coast and showered the land — sometimes violently, sometimes gently. And even now, out in the bright cold, the wide beauty that only this river could give all flowed, all somehow worked in a magnitude far greater than us. The land, the reality of the elements temporarily eclipsed the hard tragedy and brutality of our humanness.

I glanced back at Jasper who steered the boat. The black man sat beside him, sloppily sipping and warming his hands with the mug. In their eyes was the same watery weariness from the cold. Yet I could see them both scanning tree lines and marshheads for ducks or signs of other game. Maybe they were thinking of summer, too.

UNIMPROVED PROPERTY

We were driving out Shearson's Bluff Road, and for a while, dipping into a slight bottom, we hit a spot where the woods closed in and narrowed the passage, the way it used to be the whole trip out to the river. Then we came out into the new right of way, straight, elevated, only clean grass for fifty feet on either side, feeding into the subdivisions, the condominiums, the apartments with row upon row of units, and the trees now

stranded in small groups in backyards or bunched into
cul-de-sacs. It looked hot, and I started to chew my lower
lip, thinking about how the live oak, the black tupelo,
sweetgum, and pines had once shaded that narrow, twisting road.

I remembered how it had been when I had pedaled
down the road on my bicycle. In the late mornings with
the air still cool and thick in the trees, the forest had
massed around me as if I were riding down a tunnel that
glowed from within. Back then it was fun to look for the
small ditches and creeks—the modest slits in the great,
secure walls of trees. Often I would stop and explore,
finding frogs or sometimes snakes in the ditches, fiddler
crabs and pools with shiners in the creeks.

Only ten years before, Shearson's Bluff had still been a
settlement of black fishermen and tradesmen that had
stretched for about two miles along the road towards the
bluffs and marshes to the east. There were well-built,
modest houses on narrow sand lanes that wove through the
deep woods like tributaries to the marshes and tidal flats.
Because I had lived nearby in the summers, I had known
many of its people and spent a lot of time growing up at
Shearson's.

Even before that, before my birth, long before my time
and greatly embellished in my mind because I had never

lived it, were the memories drawn from the stories my mother would tell—her family's day trips from town with huge picnics, stopping to buy shrimp or crabs from the fishermen at Shearson's in late morning, sometimes talking with old men or women in rockers or shirtless children until noon. Then hurrying to make lunch at her cousins', spreading blankets on the bluff overlooking the deep water and eating boiled shrimp and ham sandwiches with chutney and butter, drinking tea boiled with sassafras, and soda cake for dessert. Most of the day that remained was spent riding in the open car back through the dense tunnel of live oaks, and her family would get back to town, exhausted, at dusk.

Once again, after we crossed a tiny creek over an old concrete bridge, there was another hundred yards or so where the wide right of way narrowed and the woods came back to hold the road. It gave me a calm, private feeling to pass here. Then there was the old hairpin turn, and you could see how it had been cut off with another large right of way to make a smooth turn, like the hypotenuse of a triangle to the old elbow. I turned my head and stared down toward the severed portion of road. I remembered it, and if I had been driving I would have stopped. Since this was not possible I thought about the old church sheltered in the turn and how it looked, through the pines and oaks, eastward, across an expanse of lime green marsh. When the slaves had come off the island plantations they had come to Shearson's Bluff to live. The church had been built on the spot where they had landed as free men.

I thought about Rachel's house, a few hundred yards north of the church. From her porch you could only catch glimpses of marsh and the water beyond, but there was something pleasantly tantalizing about that and you could always feel the breeze when you sat on her porch. Rachel was the cook of a good friend of mine. She had been dead for ten years.

We were traveling quickly along the wide, new right of way, and now there were subdivisions and spotty trees and heat and cars all the way to the end, where I'd heard they'd built a new marina. Closer to the end, nearer the deep water, the houses in the new subdivisions began to be larger. There were a few more trees, and the lots looked to be closer to a half acre than a quarter acre in size. We began to slow down, and the real estate agent who was driving the car began to talk.

"These last five subdivisions there on the left and right are really the best, upscale." He gestured with a quick sweep of his hand as if he were sowing seeds. "Should we just turn in and look through them all—to give you a sense of the place—or do you want to go straight to my listings?"

"Whatever you think," I said. "It doesn't take long to get a feel for this place."

"Well then, let's drive up the road a piece to my subdivisions," the agent said, looking at his watch.

"Shearson's Bluff Plantation," one entry sign read; "Marshview," another; "Live Oaks," yet another. The last sign had been sandblasted in order to make the wood look weathered. Some landscape architect had planted river birches and juniper in precise, round patches in front of the sign. I had seen almost the same plantings in front of new subdivisions up in New Jersey. We turned in.

"Most of these homes," the agent said, "are Low-country style."

A few of them had good porches, but there was something too new and at the same time worn-out about them. Everything was clipped and clean. The lots seemed too small and open, and the most prominent feature of every house was the concrete driveway, with the cars and boats and RV's. There was no dirt, none of the soft, gray, sifted dirt I remembered from the barefoot summers when I explored Shearson's with my friend.

"We're starting to use vinyl siding on some of the specs I'm building in the next subdivision. I swear I can't tell the difference until I'm right up on it. You talk about a maintenance-free product. It'll be here long after we're gone. Let's go take a look!"

"Is there anything by itself?" I asked with a sigh. "You know, an acre or two on the edge of all this, still sort of in the woods, maybe on the marsh?"

"Not much," the agent said, seeming a bit disappointed. "It would build out more expensive, too, a custom home."

"Let's see it."

"I've got a twenty-two hundred square foot Low-country style cottage at the end of this cul-de-sac," the agent said, then stopped, assuming an air of great gravity. "I'd like you to see the quality construction. I want you to walk it, get a feel for the community." Again, he made a sweeping gesture with his hand, as if by some force he were creating something more than could be seen.

"Sorry, but I'd like to see the land now."

"All right," the agent said. We made a quick U-turn and were soon headed back down Shearson's Bluff Road. I was depressed now. On the ride out, there was still too much shock. Also there was the hope that somewhere along the road, near the end or on some edge, there would still be a bit of the old community with the thick, tight trees and the well-built wooden cottages, each colorful, each a bit different, each having a large front porch with the old people rocking and talking, opulent plants along the railings and trellises and mimosas (considered now a weed tree) in the yards. And there would always be shrimp nets hanging from the low branches, bateaus being worked on, garden plots and lazy dogs in the soft, raked-clean dirt with patches of sun through the thick trees. But when you see something twice and from the opposite direction, the entirety of it sets in.

"How long have you been away?" the agent asked, trying to break the tight silence that had set in.

"Twelve years."

"I bet you're glad to be coming back. I hear New York is a real mess. I was reading an article that said a one-bedroom condo in the city costs over a hundred-fifty thousand. Is that for real?"

I nodded, then said, "Where is this land?"

"Off the old hairpin turn up here. It's on the eastern side of the road and has a marsh view and frontage."

I didn't say a thing, but I began to feel a tingly sense of excitement and dread in my stomach.

"The piece is expensive, I'll be honest with you. Overpriced, I think. The view is good for marsh-front. But, well, you'll see . . . got a couple of drawbacks."

We banked off the road, bumping over a culvert, a stretch of dirt and gravel, bouncing down now onto the old pavement, bumpy from the roots of the trees at the edges. Without a doubt now, I knew we were going to pass the church and Rachel's house, and I began to brace myself for it. Tragic and sad and final as it was to see the rest of Shearson's cut up and changed, I had somehow accepted it. For the last five years or so I'd been hearing about the subdivisions and the new marina. But the church and her house, I did not want to confront these, hoping by some magic that they would remain as I remembered them.

"As you can see, this is all fairly prime property. High, well drained."

"I know the land."

"Oh, really?"

So far, with the old road, it was as if time had stopped. The live oaks arched and vaulted and hung over the imperfect pavement and then the gums and pines, rattly palmettoes, mimosas melded in the background, wrapped heavily by wild grape-vine, wisteria here and there, fragrant with honeysuckle. They made the late morning air glow an ionized gold. I could begin to see the turn, which was lit up with the green expanse of marsh behind it. I wanted to roll down the windows and feel the thick humidity of the air, hear the slow blur of the cicadas. I knew that the church would be on the other side of the turn if it were still there, and then, a fifth of a mile or so, Rachel's house. I felt sick at the thought of seeing the place in shambles, or with twenty condominiums and people with tennis rackets in its place. Better a ruin, I thought.

We rounded the turn and the agent slowed, arching his arms around the wheel, leaning forward. I was frozen at first, then I jumped forward. The church was there! Just as it had always been—white clapboard a foot wide; bright green trim and shutters; the pitched, stand-and-seam roof, silver, bleeding small stains to the eave. I was amazed, and suddenly happy. The paint was dull and chipped, but it was still there. You could tell the place was still being used. I began to notice things that I'd forgotten. Two huge live oaks reached around from behind the church like great brown arms, and three umbrellalike loblollies stood proudly in front. The six columns of the high entrance stoop were at least forty feet—single pieces of rough-sawn heart pine, simple and square, strong, not quite finished. The parking lot was a combination of fine white sand and Bermuda grass and had no real definition beyond that of the shade of overhanging trees.

Slowly I began to detect the motion of the car again. And then Rachel's house was in front of me, and with her neighbor's, Robert Spenser's, they were almost exactly as they had been, with the random camellias and azaleas and palmettoes out front, lush, slightly misshapen and unkempt. In the side yards, straight rows of okra, squash, and field peas stretched to the trees. There was even a child's bicycle in front of Rachel's.

We stopped a short way past her house. We were almost at the other end, where the cut-off hairpin once again banked up and joined the new right of way. I could see the tops of cars whizzing by. The agent now pointed to the other side of the road. A small dirt path wove into a nicely wooded plot. I could see the glow of the marsh through it, and I could still see Rachel's on the other side. The church was just out of sight.

The agent hunched up over the wheel now and pointed to the land. Then, with the same gravity he'd used before, he motioned his head towards Rachel's house and the neighbor's and the church.

"I think you may have noticed why I think this land is overpriced." His voice sounded fast with the rush of air-conditioning pouring through the vents. "The owner of all this is the church. (It's a big church. Lot of 'em.) Right when things started to move out here, they bought these few pieces around them. One was out of an estate, I think. A few more they bought from members who were having trouble holding on. Rented them back. Now we are hearing they may have overextended themselves. Still have a good many members, but lots have moved. They put this piece up for sale about a year ago. Must still have some capability, because they haven't budged on price. I've brought them a few fair offers."

"They own all of this?" I pointed to the lot, then swung around and looked down the road towards Rachel's house and the church.

"Yeah," the agent said, his eyes resting on Rachel's house. "It's what I was trying to tell you. Nothing against the church, but it's hard to sell a tract that sits across from such unimproved property. I didn't think you'd be interested; something out here's just not right as it sits, doesn't seem cleaned up enough."

The thoughts started racing through my mind, now. I thought of Rachel's funeral in that very church, and the hundred and fifty black people who attended, and the few, privileged whites—parts of three or four families. We were seated up front behind Rachel's two sisters and cousins. There were black satin ribbons tied around the tops of the balcony columns.

The singing was as strong as the exposed beams and rafters of the church, needing only the melody of a single piano to carry the rifts, as soft and as beautiful and as powerful as the breeze through the marsh and trees. And then the young, well-groomed preacher in his starched collar started saying, after almost every person in the congregation had gotten up and said a simple farewell to Rachel, "Rachel was a solid person; she held herself well. She was a clean person. She had a clean life. Every time I walk by her yard, it was raked up clean. Every time I pass her garden, it was hoed out. Her front porch was scrubbed down and she always call you to come sit and talk if you passing. She was a good neighbor." And then stopping and looking squarely at Rachel in the coffin, "Sister Rachel, you had pain in the end, but now He taken it from you. Rachel, you go on now and take your rest, we all loved you, but Jesus loves you best."

"You see that house there?" I was suddenly yelling at the agent. My fist and pointed finger struck past his face. *"You see Rachel's house?* It was always clean, you understand. I knew her; I have friends who even knew her better. I ate in her kitchen many a time. It was a privilege to do that, you see. Have you ever seen a woodstove? Have you ever had to wait for a pot of grits to simmer? Ever tasted a rabbit stew that cooked all day?"

The agent drew back in amazement. He turned his head towards the house and peered at it as if he were looking beyond it.

"You see that porch?" I asked. "Ever sat on a front porch with only the breeze and one beer and an old black lady's stories — for two-three hours! What makes you think her porch wasn't clean? Ever helped hoe a garden or fixed a hen house? Ever felt that powder soft dirt between your toes? What makes you think this place isn't the best as it sits now? To hell with it! Enough of your improved property!"

The agent's amazement suddenly soured, and was quickly replaced by a tightness around his temples, a slight flare to his nostrils. "You interested in this land or not? I'm not going to waste my time getting preached to about shacks and dirt lots. It's all right for you blue bloods to have summer houses on the best deep-water property in this county. And then you want all this that's between for your old, storybook niggers and maids. What about the rest of us? Where do we live? I can afford a two-hundred-thousand-dollar home. Where do I build it?" He pointed at the land. "Are you interested or not? There it is. Hundred and twenty-five thousand. Only money will buy it now, my friend. One point seven acres. One hundred and three feet of marsh frontage. Average elevation fourteen point five feet. No water. No sewer."

I let out a long breath. I felt a sudden impulse to go back to New York. "I don't know," I said. "I'll have to think. I'll have to come back later and walk around."

"You think about it," the agent snapped. He put the car

in gear and started to accelerate towards the new right of way. "Think hard, too. It won't be around forever."

We stopped, then bumped up onto the new, wide road.

"Every time I build another house out this way, every time we cut another road and bring sewer and water another hundred yards, taxes bump up another notch. Makes it mighty hard for some people to hold on to their unimproved property, mighty hard . . ."

I could feel the hard acceleration down the new road and he was still talking.

". . . what are you worried about anyway? They all make good money when they sell. Damn good money. You should see the cars. Some of them can even afford to send their children to private school . . ."

You could hear the sighing of the breeze through the marsh, the trees and the saw palms below like a sonorous chant welcoming the coolness that came from the sea. I was amazed at how well that sound could muffle the noise of the cars passing on the elevated right of way a few hundred yards to the west.

The land of the lot sloped down into a six-foot bluff and the marsh stretched out in front of me like a fanning ocean. It had always been a reflex of mine to draw a deep breath whenever I stood in front of such a salt marsh. Looking back through the trees, I could barely see the top of my rental car, which was parked on the edge of the old road.

I began to try to picture a clearing in the lot, then a house in the clearing. Then what kind of house and how much yard and which trees to leave and which trees to take out. But this quickly became difficult because I only wanted to listen to the breeze, and then the swaying motion of the moss and branches and leaves and fronds began to give the impression that the whole lot was alive, moving with the same easiness of someone shifting in their sleep or rocking on a porch.

Finally, I focused on a rather clear spot near the middle of the lot. "Clear only enough for the house and leave the rest and let the branches of the oaks rub the roof," I said to myself and then stopped. At that same instant, moving and craning the same way an egret will step through a shallow creek, I saw a young black boy headed across the lot towards the marsh to my east. He would often stop, bend down and pick up something, then resume. He had a large paper sack in one hand and I could see the chicken neck stains coming through the paper. He carried a dip net across his shoulder and small wooden basket. He stopped for quite a while in the very clearing I had been contemplating for the house, then moved into the shadows and was gone, blending into the murmuring mass of the forest, fading as if on the edge of a dream. I caught myself lurching forward to run after him, but stopped. I then stood for a very long time.

Finally I turned once again to the expanse of marsh which was bent, fluid, and now golden. I became glad that the boy hadn't seen me and that I hadn't called out to him. I probably would have frightened him, I thought. Even here, they probably have to teach all of them not to talk with strangers these days. I watched a small group of herons beating their way awkwardly against the stiff breeze; finally, they gave up, turning downriver, landing on a piece of mud flat yet to be covered by the tide.

"It's time to go now," I said out loud to the breeze, the bluff, the property. And as I walked back through the woods to the car, I began to imagine the peaceful little creek the boy was going to crab. It was amazing how clearly I could picture it all: him setting the handlines with excitement and care, then waiting and finally dipping the crabs and putting them in the basket. And on the way back, cool-gray, almost dark with the aroma of the marsh and the breeze that slowed and thickened with moisture, he was still exploring the bluff, probably walking over the very place I had just stood. And with no noise at all, there he was, covering my tracks with the prints of feet that same worn color of the soft, clean dirt.

TWO MOONS

In the east the stars were thinning out as if some great hand had taken a rag doused in turpentine and brushed the line of the horizon. Over the dust-green glow of the tachometers and pressure gauges, the aqueous red of the compass bowl, Gerard abandoned his guide star and concentrated on the compass-card.

Tucking his chin down into the V of his parka, he found the string of the hood with his mouth, chewing, the knot softening, tasting salty. It should be as good as I remember, he thought, a throbbing excitement building in his lower stomach with the vibration of the engines. There is nothing now but the simple things. He had been telling himself that for the last seven months, ever since he'd left Melissa.

The wind was fresh, slightly chilly from the early April water, and they moved in a gently forwarding motion, engines a zesty wail. The ocean was almost flat, yet with twilight he could feel it pick up, see a grayish whitecap here and there. It was a fair southeaster, though, and he knew it would abate as the sun gained power.

He yawned, then stood up rather quickly, rocking onto the balls of his feet to warm himself up. The boat felt like it fit him as he sized up its lines and curves from the bridge above. With the breeze, the cords began to tingle and clang in the superstructure, drawn into vibrant flutter, only to abandon to a lone and hollow rapping. The repetition of that one sound suddenly caused him to sit down and lose his concentration. For a moment he was unable to detect the forward motion of the boat.

An August afternoon's nap had made him leave Melissa. It was odd, too, because for more than a year he had felt himself gaining a fuller grip, excitingly being pulled closer to her, closer to something else that had a magnitude he couldn't comprehend.

He had been in love with only one woman before Melissa, and that woman, at the end of college, with an accepted proposal of marriage, had left him. At the time he had given little thought to what marriage was. He had just proposed, only thinking of it as a logical next step, a chance to become more deeply wrapt in the excitement of love. It was a means to find out more about her—the sole object of his passion.

He had never heard from her again. The initial pain of that loss had stifled him; he had focused, concentrated all his being into that one relationship, that one person, only to have it dissolve instantly, with no notice. A strange desire to start fishing had overtaken him then. He began to long for the lost excitement and challenge of possessing a person fully, and he imagined that hunting for those magnificent and powerful billfish on the lush waters of the stream was a simple substitute. But only one month later, he had seen Melissa.

It was June. She stood sideways to him as he entered the garden at a friend's cocktail party. She was a looker: strong athletic hips and shoulders, smooth and pressed tightly against her linen dress, her hair thrown back, tickling her tanned neck as the breeze, dusk-viscosity of water, moved it. There was a small gibbous mark right above her eye. Upon seeing it, he kept looking at it, concentrating. For a while, he thought it was a fleck of a leaf or a small bug, but then he realized it was permanent —a scar of some sort, of some past that he suddenly thirsted for; part of her. Excited, he used his first conception of it as an impetus to move.

"Is that a bug over your eye?" He nodded his head, reddening.

"I would know that." She smiled. "It's a scar, a rock thrown by some bully when I was three."

"Oh," he said thrusting his hand into his pocket, biting the edge of his glass. "Doesn't hurt, does it?"

"No."

"Good," he said. "Because it's beautiful."

She flushed, lighting up, her coppered forehead gleaning the run of blood below. Seeing her in the scent of the honeysuckle that billowed from the wall, seeing her looking at him through that blue-gray part of dusk which cicadas seemed to coax, phase by phase, into night, he suddenly felt energized. At that very instant the lost woman was gone and he was boldly moving forward again. This would be the one, he knew, if he worked at it.

At first, Melissa had to get out of another relationship. That almost made it better. They would talk in the square at lunch, or meet secretly at her cottage at the beach. He felt nervous, at times exasperated, but always fresh and excited, pursuing. That fall she had a semester of school and was away. His love for her grew even more, fearing that she might not come back, yet sensing she would return—bigger, fuller, enhanced by the longings and workings of his mind.

And that spring she was home, and the second summer they were together, alone. They went out at night, caught white shrimp in the estuaries with cast nets and Coleman lanterns, sautéing them at dawn in butter and cracked pepper and eating them on the porch of her cottage with the first light's breeze beginning to move. They would both go to work, swim in the afternoons, crab and fish the beaches and small, domestic rivers, and make love in the evenings. Soon it became a comfortable, predictable cycle.

It was as if the nap on that August afternoon were the height of it all. The breeze that came in through the blinds cooled them in sleep, clapping the cords and slats against the window's edge. This wind was the first of the fall northeasters that seemed to bring back the blue skies of spring.

A gust whipped through the screen, and he opened his eyes to see the blinds furled out like a tongue, drop to tap, rap. He knew it was a breeze of the sea. The way it moved over his body felt like a cool and lightly drawn strip of emery cloth running up the hairs of his thighs and chest . . . and the smell, the cool. He imagined her doing it with her tongue.

There was another gust, then the peaceful flapping which made him swallow, wiggle down his shoulders, and drape his arm over the small of her back. He could feel her warmth, and in her sleep, she nestled her leg towards him, purring.

He looked up again at the blinds and the moving barlike shadows they cast on the bed. He heard the rhythmic rap-tapping. Then through the blinds, low in the eastern afternoon sky, he saw the pale summer's moon. Seeming to materialize the way a deer will in the forest, it shocked him. It was almost full, the color of wet cotton. He kept focusing on it, transfixed. So delicate, so close, so beautiful he felt he could reach out and bring it into the bed with them. It was then he knew he had her, and that sole moon was a symbol of their bond.

He was going to wake her to love her again, but looking once again at the faint moon and the blue strips of sky through the shades, his head turned sideways, something hit him.

It was the bigness that for so long he had wanted, that for so long he had believed he couldn't touch—the same inexplicable magnitude of feeling that hangs in the corners of your dreams, that hums in the smell of turned dirt

on a moist April morning or trails the distant shrieks and
shouts of children playing in leaves on autumn afternoons.
Now it was there, swept into the room, swirling, expanding around him and amplifying in the idiom of the present
—something of the breeze, the falling light, the rhythmic
tapping and swishing of wind through late summer screens,
the warmth of bodies and wisping coolness of sea air, the
peace of half-slumber and the beckoning vastness of that
faint moon over blue ocean skies. He began to feel dizzy
as if the sensation, coded in him long ago, were passing
vividly through him then taking form: embodied, his to
hold, his to have. . . .

But what next? He had found himself suddenly sitting
up right in the bed, breathing heavily. It was as if his
vision had closed in completely, and he could see no more
with her, as if marriage, instead of being a deeper excitement and discovery, might very well be a total stagnation.
What more could there be? His thoughts began to quicken
with panic, and he began to lose the excitement to panic.
It was then that he began to fidget in the secure bed
beside Melissa—the sole object of his passion.

With the cool smell of the sea coming through those
shades, his concentration began to shift like the ebbing of
a flood tide. Maybe I'll just fish, he thought. It's got to be
simple there. It was the first time he'd thought about the

excitement of blue marlin since the departure of the other woman, and now he started to want it.

With his inheritance (with which, only a month before, he had planned to buy a house after they got married) he bought a boat — a secondhand, but well-kept, Bertram 31. It had twin 440 Chryslers; gusty four-barrel carburetors; low, slick lines; good beam, fast. Fall and winter he worked on the boat, outfitting it in Miami with the best equipment — Rybovich outriggers and fighting chair bolted through the hull, new teak, all chromium hardware, pipe welder's tuna tower, and all the electronics and radar.

In February he came back up the waterway and found a small port, Palmetto, Florida, close enough to Jacksonville, so the chartering business would be good, secluded enough, so he could keep to himself and fish how he wanted. Although the season was short, it was a good coast for marlin.

For the rest of the winter he lived on the boat and worked and concentrated on little things — studying the loran charts, finding good trenches and ridges and plotting courses to them, twisting leader wires and experimenting on new baits. The excitement seemed to build each late winter day, the sun's angle bearing down more directly, bringing the fair southwesters which held moist gulf air. There were great storms. Sometimes he paid little attention to them, only stayed in the warm cabin of the boat, reading, plotting, focusing only on his work. Or sometimes he confronted the storms, taking his boat offshore into the white water. With the work, the concentration, and anticipation he would tell himself how wonderful it all was. Only at certain times would he seem to falter and think of Melissa. A few times a sensation close to dizziness would seem to spin on him from above, seeming to say, "What have you done? What are you doing? Where are you going? What will happen next?" And he would cut himself off just as he began to think that he'd missed something with her, that there had been something right out in front of them—something more—that he simply couldn't see.

Even though the sea was still picking up, he nudged the throttles forward a bit, gaining 2,000 rpms on each engine. He knew the boat could easily take it and he was eager to get his baits in the water.

Looking back at the wake, he could see the furious twin columns of phosphorescence jetting back from the wheels, an intermittent, soundless but lush explosion of green as they ran over jellyfish.

A tap on his shoulder made him start. Jackson handed

him a cup of coffee. "Thought you might need this all alone up here in the chill."

"Thanks." Gerard took the cup. "You finished with the baits?"

"Had to leave that big tuna, with this chop picking up. Liked to sewed my finger up in his belly," Jackson, the mate, said, shivering a bit. "I'll get to him when we shut down."

"Good." Gerard motioned Jackson to sit down on the bench beside him. "What do you think of the charter?"

"Says he's fished for sails in West Palm and Cozumel," Jackson said.

"That's a good start," Gerard said. "But sails aren't marlin. You keep an eye on him. Remember what I said about losing fish." Jackson nodded as he put his hands in his parka.

It was beginning to get light now. Gerard could make out Jackson's features. He had a wide jaw and blond beard, blue eyes the color of the Gulf Stream. In coloring, he looked very much like Gerard himself. They were both about the same age. But Jackson was thicker, looked more solid and steady, with truer eyes.

From the day Gerard hired him, he had been pleased with him. Jackson was a natural with baits, rigging Spanish mackerel and mullet simply but with incredible dexterity, sewing the hooks into their bellies with the quick strokes of a surgeon. He always worked and knew how to do most everything. One day he would polish all the chrome and oil the teak on the boat; the next day he would reset the drags on all the reels. He could tune the engines, change oil, and even fix minor problems with the electronic gear. There was something in the way that Jackson directed his energy, fearlessly spreading it out, that interested Gerard, at times made him envious. Perhaps the only thing he didn't like about Jackson was the way he always talked about his family—his wife and young boy. Although Jackson had no real education and had grown up on shrimp boats and charter boats, he sometimes felt that Jackson was someone that he himself could have been.

By the time they reached the Gulf Stream, the sun had been up for nearly an hour. A large weed line—the color of ripe banana peel—snaked and gently rose and fell to either side of their course. It marked the edge. Over the line, because the wind was blowing parallel to the current of the Stream, the water was slick and rolled as if coated with a film of oil. He stood up and drew in a deep breath of pollen-scented air, cool, full, the smell of crushed watermelon rind. Down-throttling evenly, he gave the brisk command, "Let's get 'em fishing," clapping his hands twice. From the breeze, the fine mist of a topped white-cap, he felt energized once again. This was what he had waited for. It was what he remembered — the purity and simplicity, the spontaneity that he knew he could never lose. They turned south, broadsiding the line of gulf weed, and he felt a shiver of delight, the sun warm on his shoulders and the back of his neck. Taking off his shirt, he started squaring things away up top.

Jackson hustled in the cockpit, head down and directed, getting things done quickly yet without noticeable clamor. Suddenly, the rods were out of the cabin, in the holders, the baits, warming in the sun of the transom; and as he leaned over to swing the outriggers into place, the baits were already being dropped back, stiff at first, turning, then diving in the white water of the wake.

Looking forward, he brought the boat up to trolling speed, synchronizing the engines by ear, lengthening the vibrations into one constant throb, then nothing but the sputter of the exhaust out through the water as they came into the troughs. He switched on the VHF radio. It crackled and clattered with blue-gum jargon of the other fishermen. He didn't listen to the words, though, only the sounds, the strange whines and airskips somehow blending with the engines, the increasing heat, the long rolling of his boat.

To starboard he found a break in the weed line and crossed there into the slicker stream-blue water so the baits wouldn't snag the grapelike clusters of sargassum weed. Only fifty yards on that side, the line of the fathometer dipped, marking out a six-fathom cliff. Just as it bottomed, he turned the boat parallel to it and the weed line and started weaving over the trough, south. Feeling set, he turned to watch the baits, taking a wide stance and bumping his hips from rail to rail with the seas, the steering wheel against his lower back and steadied with his hand.

The three baits had limbered. The two Spanish on either rigger were running perfectly, lapping on their sides as they went down the slight rollers, then diving, taking short, weaving hops as they went up the next wave, simulating the movement of a wounded fish which would catch the eye of some marlin below, if it were close. The mullet on the flat swam right behind the white water and was rigged with a one-ounce bullet sinker under its mouth, causing it to run four inches under the surface, its tail fluttering. He could see a thready line of bubble behind it.

Jackson threw in the two teasers that Gerard had made out of a baseball bat and had covered with yellow and green reflective tape to look like a dolphin. They churned and waggled in the white water, chopping. Herb Glenn, the charterer, settled into the chair, pulling on his gloves while Jackson draped the fighting harness over his shoulders. The two of them kept their eyes on the baits from below.

As Gerard was about to turn forward to scan the fathometer, the starboard teaser came out of the water, batted into the air as high as the tip of the rods. A silver-blue flash cut in on the mullet, the wahoo razoring it, clipping it off right behind the hook. The fish rolled to the rigger, slashed the bait, and hooked up on the Spanish, rod bending, line singing. Gerard slowed slightly, and after a short but frantic initial run, Herb brought it in quickly on the eighty-pound test.

In what seemed one continuous motion, Jackson wired the fish in, clubbed it, and slung it into the fish well, where it clattered twice against the side and then was quiet in the ice. Immediately, Jackson had two more baits on and was washing down the blood that had splattered the deck.

Gerard nodded at the catch, the confluence of angler and mate in action. An excellent practice round, he thought. It was a nice thirty-pound fish, and it would satisfy the charterer's desire for meat.

"That was too fast," Herb yelled up at Gerard. "Nice

fish, but too fast on this heavy tackle. No fight. I'm a sportsman."

Gerard suppressed a frown and hollered, making his voice squeaky, enthusiastic. "You want blue marlin, don't you? It's what we're out here for. You wait. You hook into one; it'll wear you out. You'll need every bit of that eighty-pound line. You wait, you'll see."

Herb got a soda and settled back in the chair, saying something to Jackson, whose chest and legs looked greased with washed-off fish slime and brine.

"Jackson." Gerard turned the boat back towards the weed line. "Could you bring me a Coke, please?"

Jackson scuttled up quickly and clung to the ladder, hooking his elbow through the rung, panting, flecks of wahoo blood like freckles on his nose and cheeks.

"Listen," Gerard said. "Big baits from now on—two good Spanish on the riggers and run a tuna on the flat. Shake off wahoos unless they're real big. We'll rig a small mullet on a fifty that we can throw at some dolphin later, during the lull. We can't be messing . . ."

The rigger pin clicked like somebody snatching a pen from a top pocket. Jackson was already moving down the ladder, and Gerard could see the marlin turned, brownish blue-silver, arcing into a boil of white water, crossing the wake. Herb gaped, frozen in the chair.

"Get it!" Gerard yelled. "Drop it back. Right rigger. Good fish."

Herb didn't move, and Gerard kept yelling from his high and hopelessly distant perch. "Get it! Drop it back! Son-of-a-bitch!"

Before Jackson could get to the line to free-spool it, the fish had taken all of the belly. The line drew tight, sung and pinged, hook thrown back to the side, bait shucked off, fish gone in two sustained and accelerating greyhounds, scared from the popping of the hook.

Gerard turned forward and stared at the expanse of glassy sea ahead, dizzy. For an instant it was if someone had thrown a switch inside that unleashed a painful complexity of emotion. What in the hell am I doing out here? he began to think. There will be more. He made himself say it.

Gerard shook his head. "That was a four, five-hundred-pound fish, Mr. Glenn. Good fish. Eater."

Jackson said nothing, only moved, head down, from the chest to the rods, putting on the larger baits. Herb cussed under his breath, scratched his head, and fumbled for a cigarette, sitting on the edge of the chair.

Gerard had caught hold of himself and thought it wise to try to encourage the charterer. "Look, Herb, now you've got one to learn from. Blues are faster and more powerful than sails. There will be more. It's good out here."

The sky was now that deep spring morning blue, air pure and moving softly yet confidently. He sighted down the weed line and saw the bobbing white-gray and amber flecks of birds as they worked over it. He angled the boat that way. Nearer, he could see they were over fish, and then, in quick succession as if thrust from a toaster, two dolphin came out, hanging six feet out of the water, arcing bright green-yellow, dropping back.

"Look sharp on that right rigger, Jackson, Herby. Something under dolphin up here."

From the tower, he could see the school, bunching as shadows under the rectangular shade of a glossy sheet of plywood. Another fish came out, skipping at a shallow, quick angle, its green, bull head smacking, almost audible in front of the sound of the engines. A deeper shadow lay, immobile, behind the school.

"Good fish, Jesus Christ, good fish!" he shouted. "Look sharp on that rigger."

As they passed the school he turned, watching the marlin shift and angle slowly up behind the lapping bait. For what seemed long minutes, there was only the showering of the engines, the wild pulsing of blood in his

head, the twitching of the arms. Jackson perched on
his toes, bent forward next to the rod; Herb strained
out of the chair. The fish lay like a submarine under
the bait, the tip of its tail barely slitting the surface,
moving in sluggish arcs. Its bill came out, waggling over
the bait, only to drop back, sink, and hang as a colorless shadow.

"Got a looker! What a looker!" Gerard felt a rush of
adrenaline, knowing that such a fish, not so hungry from
probably having eaten a dolphin, could hang like that for
twenty or thirty minutes, even switch from bait to bait,
leery. He wondered why such a fish would leave its school
and come behind the boat anyway. The main thing now
was to keep everything constant and quiet and let the fish
decide for itself. It was a magnificent fish, maybe eight
hundred pounds, silver-brown from the top with the girth
of a torpedo. It was a female.

They must have trolled for another ten minutes with the
fish finning lazily behind the bait.

The marlin began to fade into the deep like the receding shadow of a cloud having just whisked over the sun.
Then suddenly from the depths, it made a spurt, gills
flared, lighting up from the massive intake of oxygen and
raised body temperature of the frenzy. The bars on its side
glowed blue, like potent neon. Its bill slashed the bait,

and it crashed, grabbing the Spanish from underneath, rolling, tearing off.

"Jackson!" Gerard yelled. "You make sure Herb hooks him up."

The mate had already grabbed the rod and was dropping it back, the clicker whining in spurts that blended into a constantly accelerating crescendo. Keeping his thumb on the spool, pointing the tip of the rod at the fish, Jackson moved to the chair where Herb was ready. Then he set the butt in the gimbel and instructed Herb to strike it. At the same time, Gerard gunned the boat forward. Herb jabbed the fish four more times, setting the hook.

The marlin came out, tailwalking through the gulf weed, chips of it flying off of its massive silver-black head. It ripped off more line, greyhounding, skipping off the water the way misfired bottle rockets will hit a river. Furling down into the water on its side, seeming to suck in a torrent of spray and foam with it, it went under. The monofilament line crackled and whined.

"Ease up on it a bit," Gerard yelled.

Herb moved the drag, the small release of pressure spiriting the fish, making it come out in a big-shouldered wag to the tip of its tail, hang, and slap heavily on its silver side. It was up again and again, boiling farther away on the surface, keeping airborne by incredible thrusts of its tail.

At the end of this display, which had Jackson whooping, slapping his hat on his leg, Gerard scurried down from the bridge and took the station in the cockpit, immediately jamming the throttles into reverse, backing down into the seas with sheets of spray slapping over the transom. Jackson strapped Herb in, and he worked in quick pumps, gaining line.

The point now was to try and get the fish to the transom before it sounded. Gerard had not always fished like this. In fact, it was by no means the most sporting way, for the boat and the eighty-pound test did a tremendous amount of the work. Before, when he fished with his father, they had used fifty-pound tackle and had only backed to keep the transom facing the fish. In that way, after the initial aerial battle the marlin would sound for the long fight in which angler and fish would give and take line for hours and then, if the fish were hooked properly in the top of the bill and sharks hadn't gotten it, it would finally break, ending its fight in two of three languid jumps within fifty yards of the boat, sometimes even close enough to be wetted by the spray. All its energy gone, the fish would usually come voluntarily, finning on its side, accepting the hands on the leader, then around its bill, the tagging above its pectoral fin and release from which it would hang and then swim calmly away. Nevertheless, fishing that way, with patience and time, you would sometimes lose them.

But now, since he had decided to make fishing his life, he was more interested in applying maximum power against the fish's. In doing that and repeating it, he hoped to take more from the fight, sustain the intensity. He wanted the fish to be alive and full of beauty, bigness, when it was at the transom; the point where he would hit it with the gaff, join it to his boat, and in doing so kill it. This was not to say there wasn't risk in this approach, too. A fish, not hooked solidly, could throw the hook or break the line from the tremendous tension. Even more, a powerful green fish could go wild, lancing whatever stood in its way, battering and shredding both angler and boat. Maybe that is what he wanted — to live in the excitement of this possibility, to sustain the climax, to sink his gaff into the fish at the point where the power, the beauty, were greatest. As the knot of the double line came into sight, he slowed the boat, slipping it into neutral, and picked up the flying gaff from where it lay on the side of the deck.

Very quickly, with Herb blowing and pumping over the rod, the knot of the double line came through the eyes; the swivel and leader wire cut the surface as the fish thrashed near the top, batting the wire with its bill, blood now beginning to pour from its gills. In split timing,

Jackson abandoned his post behind the chair and, smoothing the gloves tight into the creases of his fingers, came to the stern with Gerard. In the second in which the fish calmed, Jackson grabbed the #16 wire, wrapping it over his knuckles in deft, twirling pulls, the wire coming over his head, twanging onto the deck in loose coils. He moved the fish to a shallow distance within reach of the gaff, then, wire clenched in both hands, dropped into a squat on the deck so the wire arched over the transom, that surface giving him the leverage to hold.

Gerard fought off waves of excitement that fluttered through his arms like someone pinching his inner elbow. He blocked out everything: all emotion, focusing and concentrating that energy into one spot behind the great fish's spread fin. As the marlin swung sideways about to jump, Gerard hit it with the gaff, digging the point in, up through the fish, pulling with all his strength. The pole detached, clanging onto the deck like a dropped can. Jackson released the wire, sprang clear, and the fish jumped against the rope, checked, a taut snapping of the backbone, the flailing out of a pinkish foam of blood.

For one full minute no one moved or said anything. They gaped at the size, the bigness, of the fish, which now slowly rolled to its side and twitched in the water.

Then Jackson's voice lit up. "Mr. Glenn, I'll bet you,

you've just caught a new state record." There was a powerful directness in the way he said it but the words meant no
more than what they meant.

"My God, what will a fish like that weigh?" Glenn
unstrapped the harness and moved towards the transom
for a better look. His whole shirt was soaked with sweat.

"Eight hundred, maybe a thousand pounds," Gerard
spoke as if in a daze, not looking at Glenn but at the fish.
Then confused, almost frantically, he grabbed the gaff
rope which secured the fish to his boat and jerked it as if
he were trying to pull something more out of the dying
fish. There was only the heavy, dead weight of the marlin.
He looked hard at the fish again and could see the color
draining from it. All at once, he let go of the rope as if
something had burned him. Maybe another minute passed
with Gerard just staring at the motionless fish, staring as
if he saw nothing in the limitless blue waters that stretched
out before him. He could barely hear Jackson as he said,
"What now? What next?"

Jackson was on the bridge at the helm, his left hand
firmly on the wheel, his right resting calmly on the throttles. The afternoon breeze had whipped the sea into a
four-foot chop. Only thirty minutes before, he had taken
the boat off autopilot and slowed a couple of thousand

rpms. Now every time they would surf down a roller, jerking into a broach at the trough, Jackson, alert, ready, would guide them back with amazing fluidity, engines barely cavitating.

Herb Glenn had stretched himself out in the fighting chair with a beer in one hand, a cigarette in the other. He finally pulled the bill of his hat down low over his eyes and began to doze.

Gerard was in the forward berth taking a nap. Before lying down, he had cracked the windshields and lowered the blinds, half closing them. They topped a roller and he woke suddenly with a jolt. Opening his eyes, he was instantly blinded by a suffocating white light from above. At first he didn't know where he was, but slowly he could feel the breeze, a gritty sheen of salt water in it. Then he started to make out the fading blue sky behind weak, barlike shadows of blinds. At last he heard the faint, rhythmic rapping of the blinds and pinging of the rigger cords over the constant showering of the engines. He rolled off the bunk and groped out of the cabin.

Stumbling over the great fish that lay across the cockpit, its bill jutting over the gunwale like a sabre, he slowly climbed to the bridge. He felt weak, confused, drained as if something had left him forever.

"Where are we?" he said to Jackson.

"About eight miles off of N-5." Jackson moved over on the bench. "Ought to be able to pick it up any minute now."

Gerard flopped onto the seat, still rubbing his eyes. With the afternoon haze, the sun arching down into their course, the thick haze of sleep around his vision like cotton, he could still barely see anything. He felt drugged and said nothing.

"That's one hell of a fish, captain," Jackson said. "You ought to have no problem keeping this boat full of charters now. Won't have to advertise either. They'll send TV cameras from Jacksonville for this 'un."

He nodded, shielding his eyes.

"You mind if I call home when we get in so I can get the wife to bring the young'un down?"

"I guess," he said softly.

"That little rat's nest of mine won't believe that fish. He'll want to crawl all over it."

"How old is he?" Gerard asked rather suddenly.

"That fish?"

"No, your boy."

"Oh, he's three and a half," Jackson said. "Got a mop a hair on his head like a five-year-old."

He found his sunglasses out of the console and put them on. "I really wouldn't have known how old he was."

"They're a mess at three, let me tell you. Should have heard him the other evening," Jackson said over the engines.

He sort of shuddered inwardly, now fully awake, not wanting to hear but interested and beginning to look hard for the first buoy and that thin purple thread of land that always looks like a mirage at first.

"Little thing was on the porch and began to holler like a fool, 'Two moons, Daddy, Mommy. Two moons! Two moons!' So we ran out there to see what he was about." Jackson began to smile and gesture wildly like the child, animated, telling the story as if he were three. "'What about the moon?' I asked him. 'Two moons, two moons,' he said again. 'Where?' Cindy asked. 'I only see one Mr. Moon.' We both looked across the river at the moon coming up. 'No, no, two moons,' He began to point. 'See dat one in the water and that on'er one up in the sky!' Now ain't that something. We were both concentrating on the moon in the sky so much, we couldn't see the one beyond it on the water. If you think about it, he was the one that had us for fools! We both had to laugh."

Gerard gave a small chuckle.

"I tell you something," Jackson said. "Them young'uns keep at it. Never stop. No way in the world you can ever figure what they'll do next."

Those last words reached him just as he could see the gibbous dot of the first buoy. He squinted hard, concentrating and focusing to pick up the land behind it. He could barely see the north end of Brady's Island, etched purple, blotty and broken.

"I'll take it now." He reached over Jackson's arm and took the wheel. "How about going down and getting me a beer?"

He eased down on the throttles with a small hopeful smile. "Two moons," he grinned. "How magnificent."

THE FIRE-EYED
STALLION—A DREAM
OF SALVATION

The snapping of tobacco was continuous. If you closed your eyes and used your imagination, there was a slight possibility of conjuring something exciting—the clattering of fire through bamboo, a distant barrage of gunfire across a plain. But as the afternoon drew on, the dry wester increased, moaning in the pines, blunting all sound; and the only thing that could best that wind was the talk of the blacks as they moved down the field pulling the tops and growth suckers from the lines of chest-high plants.

Not many white people would have been able to decipher the language of these field hands. There would be one sentence spoken in high and rapid flurries with rapid turns of Geechee dialect, and the next in a lumbering bass which seemed to capture the wide rhythms of work. An unpracticed listener might have been thrown astray like a gamboling hound behind a quick, zigzagging rabbit.

Yet, there was a definite air of sanctity in the talk, and the two elders, Larry and Cobell, seemed to know this, basking, as they paused to mop their foreheads with sweat rags, in the cadence of their words. And just before the wind muddled and then swept these phrases away, it was as if they could snatch something from the mere sound of their own voices that provided consolation out in the heat and all the work.

All the young blacks, who had finished their rows in haste, sat flaccidly under the shade oaks at the end of the field. Instead of talking they now smoked cigarettes and listened to a transistor radio that spewed the skeletal melodies of the latest pop records. As the two older hands neared the end of the row, they could hear the broken bits of music.

"We didn't do that when we was coming up, did we, Cobell?" Larry nodded towards the youths.

"No, sure didn't. We had more respect back then. We'd help our elders when we finished early." Cobell raised her voice in a feeble attempt to best both wind and music.

"Yeah, mercy." Larry said.

"And listen to that music, them blues. Those children ought to start thinking a what's ahead a them. We ain't gonna stay on this world forever. Someday we all got to pass on."

"Sure enough."

"Lord." Cobell cracked a timid smile. "But I used to listen to them blues too. I was a young'un once, and we was like them in our ways. Great day, they was some type a blues too . . . that Orleans Rag."

"That was sure enough music."

"But as sure as I stands here with both my feets in this hot sand, them blues got the debil in them and everything what's goes with that music is a part of his ways."

"That's right."

"I knows him."

"Sure enough."

"Lord, back when I was coming up," Cobell said, "I met Satan and stayed with him for quite some time. That alcohol. We used to drink cane buck come wintertime in the thick smoke of them fatwood fires and sip that sweet wine in the cool evenings of summertime. We'd come out of the fields and take to drinking. And it seemed all day in the 'bacca when we was cropping in the hot sun and our backs was paining from all the stooping we was doing to crop them lug leaves, all that would keep us going was thinking about when we'd knock off and set on the front porch and drink the sweet wine what Horace made from them scuppernong."

"Yeah, you talking. I tasted," Larry said.

"Looked like nothing would stop me off that wine and drinking and such. I still done it after I got married and had my first young'un. Seemed as though I couldn't go on without it, couldn't make it through a day without it." Cobell stopped and arched her back. The wind matted her muslin dress against her smoothly robust frame.

"Now all a this was happening to me, and I was just going on not knowing what I was doing was wrong. But the Lord has his ways, too, and He knew all along what was happening and what would happen."

"Lord has his ways, rightful enough."

"And see, the Lord was going to wait just long enough so as to make me learn a lesson, and then He was going to come in."

"Speak it, now."

"I remember I was walking down the lane one day back then, coming home from the fields, and I'd already stopped by Horace's and had me a pint bottle a wine, and I'd already drunk most a it. Now I looked down the dusty lane near Henry's fence and could see the Reverend Hines, in his suit a white, walking my way. All of a sudden, I felt real bad and throwed the bottle into the high grass and four o'clock vines what's tangled in the fence. Now when he got up to me, he stopped, and I could barely take a look at his eye. Directly, he said, 'Cobell, I ain't been seeing you around the churchyard in a long time. You better put them people down you hanging with and get around on Sundays.' And I couldn't say a word, being I felt so stifling. I just walked on to the house. All along, though, I felt real bad inside; like there was poison in me. Now if the Lord hadn't been watching over me, I wouldn't have felt that way when I saw the preacher, mercy no. I would have walked on past him, drinking that wine, blowed my liquor-smelling breath in his face, and not thought a lick. But the Lord has his ways and this is when I knows He was working on me."

"Sure enough has his ways," Larry added.

"Well, when I gets home," Cobell said, "there's a whole crowd a people on the porch, clapping that rag music, and directly I started drinking more wine and joining in on them blues. And I says to myself that I'll go to church on Sunday, while all along I'm drinking from the demi-john what's being passed around, and getting drunker.

After a while everybody left, and I starting to feeling poor again. Directly I had to lie down on the bed and by that time, that wine had me all cramp-up inside. I lay there on that pallet with the poison running up and through me in every limb of my body. About that time, I looks up at the ceiling and then I sees it."

"What that?" Larry asked, and the two had both stopped in the field with the sun drawing modest sweat from their foreheads and pitting oval stains in the centers of their backs. Cobell looked out at the thousands of pink tops of tobacco that stretched out in the field in front of her.

"Well," she said. "It was a black horse above me on the flat board of that ceiling. What they call one of them black stallions. And that horse was raised up with his feets in the air, and you could see his eyes a glittering with red fire. Seemed every time that horse would buck up, the pain and poison would shoot through me, and I got to sweating out cold on the mattress. Well I starting to crying, 'cause that horse was an evil-looking thing. After a spell, I started praying 'cause I knowed I was wrong, and I asked the Lord to help me and told him I'd change my ways if he'd ease the pain. About that time the horse left and I dropped on off to sleep."

"Mercy," Larry said. "He sure knows when to help an ailing."

"Lord knows," Cobell said. "And he helped me, and when I woke, I swore off that sweet wine and went straight to the Reverend Hines' house and told him what had happened to me. Now Reverend looked at me real serious and said that that horse was the debil with his eyes lit up red and he was out to get me until I called on the Lord and then old Satan was driven away. I started praying to the Lord lots after he told me all this. I went to church that Sunday and 'fessed to the Lord in his house and sang the spirituals all along. And I got to feeling a good warm feeling up inside a me. I be getting stronger with all that religion I was picking up on the Sabbath, and I sure didn't want no dealings with that stallion no more." She paused, fanning a leaf by her ear, vacant-eyeing the hedgerow at the end of the field. "Now I don't know what made me start back on drinking. But it happened along about four months after I saw that stallion. It was in December, if I can talk correct, but it was for sure in the wintertime because I remember the cold that year. We was picking up roots for Mr. W.D., cleaning land, and the wind blow up across that dark dirt field, and Lord, it was no place for any living soul to be. It was the only way we could get the fatwood and long pine limbs to burn in the wood stove and chimbley, though. And anyway when Mr. W.D. comes around at the house and asks us to jump in the back of his truck, wasn't much we could do, seeing we might not have a place with him that summer if we didn't. So back to what I was talking, I was going home one of those evenings with the young'uns behind me, we all toting an armful of wood, when I catches a sweet smell coming over Horace's fence with the wood smoke and then I remembered that he was making cane syrup that evening. Well, I gived my wood over to the children and told them to go at the house and set a fire. I walked around behind Horace's and sure enough they was all standing around the boiling pot, watching the mule walk around and around cranking the gears and mashing that sweet water out of the cane. And mercy, that syrup smelt good brewing down. So I walked over and stood by the fire and seen they was passing an open jar of cane buck around, what they had left over from last time. When they passed it to me, I took a long pull. It warmed me along with the glow from the popping fatwood. Now, I didn't think I was doing nothing more than keeping warm with that buck. But, directly, after I stood there for two hours or so, laughing and talking with Horace and Dolly, I began to feel the whiskey creeping up on me, so I figured I better go home. When I got in the door, I felt the poison in me again, and I was beginning to fear some. I was scared of the bed, so I stretch-out on the floor, but nothing could keep me from feeling worse. That buck was boiling up in my head and exploding in my blood. I was almost hoping I was dead. Then I looked up and saw a ring of people gathered around me on the ceiling. I was looking up at them, feeling like I was in the pit o'hell, and I started crying and praying and asking them people to help me. Now directly they started up to singing, slow and easy-like, and the music felt soft around my head. Then one of the women's what's singing reach down and put the palm of her hand all over my body-self, and where she touch, all the pain would rise out of me. The more that lady touch me the more I'd cry, and I wasn't crying because of my aching body or busting head. I was crying tears of joy, for that lady was bringing me back into the world of God, she was having pity on my soul there in the pit o'hell, even though I was a sinner, outright. Now, I knew right then that I would be one of the Lord's childrens, and since that time, I ain't studied no liquor. Paid no attention to that blues music either."

"That must a been the Lord himself in that lady what reached down for you, Cobell." Larry said.

"Sure enough was," she replied. "Ever since that night when I left all my sins in the pit o'hell and went with that lady in the ways of the Lord, I've felt like I got to make praise to Him everyday, now. All I thinks about out here is when I can get to that church and sing out to Him."

They were at the end of the row by this time. Both bent over and rubbed warm sand on their hands in an effort to take the tobacco tar off. The younger people still slumped under the oaks. Debbie and Peanut had gone off behind a windrow and sauntered back with wearied looks on their faces.

It would be another round of work before the sun would dip behind the flatwood pines, before the heat would lull and drift slowly westward, prodded softly by the cool evening darkness. Then they would all go home to the quarters, go back to the small frame houses with rusting tin roofs and bare yards, shaded by mossy oaks. The young would mingle around the pool halls, thirst for cheap wine or moonshine, then return to the houses, walking unsteadily down the dark jasmine-scented lanes, and make love violently in the stench of yellowed mattresses, impregnate without restraint, only with a wild drive to release, and somehow, in the quiet calm of night, escape from the stifling reality of the tobacco patch to which they would always return with glazed eyes and throbbing heads.

Cobell would come back, too, after a night of singing spirituals in a whitewashed church, the same distant mist coating her pupils.

As the sun began to falter in the west, the young blacks

got up and slowly joined their elders. They all turned, picked a row, and, backs to the sun, with oily hair glistening beads of bacon grease, made their way towards the other end of the field in a slow chainlike strand with the popping of the suckers ever present and the guttural flurries of dialect now blending with the wind in one blueslike intonation.

THE TWIN OAKS

I t took him ten minutes to drive from the offices at Barnett back to his farm for lunch. He would always look hard at the woods and fields on either side of the state highway. One time, a red fox as big as a hound had slunk across the road in front of him. It had stopped in a gulley just before the thicket and watched him as he passed, then bolted, the flaming white-tipped tail swallowed in last. Another day, two large does were grazing on immature sprigs of planted corn; with their copper summer coats, they stood out in relief against the foliage. For some reason they hardly even moved as he swished by, only their heads going down, then jerking up and to the side. On the county road he checked the mail, then turned through the gates, up the avenue of live oaks, to the main grounds of his farm.

There he lived alone in an old tenant house. It was wedged into a grove of pecan trees, adjacent to the big, white house that stood larger than any of the oaks that surrounded it. Its second-story porches overlooked the lawns which fell away to natural camellia and azalea gardens shaded by huge loblollies. Passing it and the hitching post out front, he pulled his truck into the full pools of shade around his little house, got out, walked across the porch and into the dark cool inside. In a few minutes he came back out, the screen door banging behind him, with a plate in one hand and a quart jar of tea in the other. Pitching his hat onto the floor, he sat down in the large rocker, leaning back, blowing out a long sigh.

For a while he only drank, pulling large gulps from the jar, rattling the ice around, drinking more. Then he picked up the tomato sandwich and took a small bite. When he was hungry it was hard merely to gnaw a quarter-sized divot from the edge, then place the sandwich back on the plate and chew carefully until all was disintegrated and washed down with the tea. But it only took the first bite, and then what was restraint grew pleasant as he tasted more and drew his meal out peacefully.

Eating, he surveyed the grounds, dappled between shade and light—the groups of trees, the lone great oaks rimmed with azaleas and camellias, the wide lawn, and the large empty house. Chewing, he shifted his gaze to an open whitewashed shed that had a chimney in its middle and was next to the woods. Beside it were the remnants of a cane mill that slanted down, abandoned and alone, gears clogged with rust and dauber nests, and the already encroaching vines—the blackberries and honeysuckle —wrapping their shoots around the rusted metal and decaying wood as if to pull them down and into the thickness of the woods.

He had seen the machine often enough. Most evenings, in the faltering light of dusk, he would look at it when he would sit after work, and the cool bluish night would come slowly from behind like sleep—a consolation, soothing his tan and warmly throbbing back. Frequently, at about the same time the pole lamp would flicker on and draw the insects into tight orbits around its globe, wood ducks would come over, the whistling black shadows, necks craning as they scanned the thick of swamp for a pothole to pitch into and roost for the night. He would usually wait for the ducks and count them. But now, as he ate, with the heat having beat the fig trees into their midday wilt, he saw more in the mill than a crumbling mass swallowed by the vines. Something caused him to think about the crude machine as he propped back in his rocker, and he began to remember when it had worked, and they had come up to the country from the city of Palmetto in the first cold of November and made syrup with it. He was six years old then.

Now the full summer lawn that spread out under the amply spaced pecans shed its soft cast, the hazy murmurings of the locusts and katydids, the smooth sounds ceasing. It was now as if it were a stage, and he could see himself—a wiry little boy with hair as white as cotton and no eyebrows—sprattling across the browned yard, sprinting towards the mill in the crisp chill of the November dusk. Old Sam had the mule and the patch of cane, and would have spent the whole day setting up the mill next to the boiler shed, so that by the time they arrived late Friday, it stood, silent and ready.

With the light draining down west, and leaving the giant oaks without color, he eyed the machine, his heavy breaths coming out white in the dusk air. It stood on rough oaken legs, massive compared to his slight frame, and there were two huge iron gears on the stand turned by a wooden pole that sloped, knotted and split, out to a twelve-foot radius. A polished leather halter hung from the end.

The mule, he thought, and smiled with excitement. "Sam's big old white mule with his floppy ears . . . he's going to have those blinder cups around his eyes." And he stood staring at the place where the animal would be, remembering how the beast looked as it plowed in a sun-baked field the summer before. Then something came slowly upon him there in the cold, with the distant wisping of a truck on the highway, the hollow, almost bell-like —"ho-ho . . . ho-ho"—of a barred owl from the deep of the swamp.

His throat felt funny, like something was pulling the plate of his mouth down into it, and he felt for the animal and the old black man. I hope that old man and that white mule never die, he thought, and almost prayed it, picturing the man in his head walking in the baggy pants, limping slightly. He felt sorry for the small gray house the man lived in, and the animal, too, no matter how huge it was. A few tears dripped down the side of his face and into the V of his neck, blurring his vision, clogging his nose.

Through the air, sharp, like the lone report of a rifle,

the screen door of the big house slapped shut, and he turned, the warm glow inside beckoning, his mother calling him for supper. Still he lingered under the mill, letting his contorted breathing find its natural rhythms, his eyes dry. Then his mother called again, and he walked slowly towards the big house, in the dark.

Always in the morning you forgot, he thought now, rocking on the porch, having finished the sandwich and taken out a penknife, scraping the dirt from under his nails. You forgot, or rather the feeling contracted into some small corner as if it were nocturnal, leery of the fresh morning light and the smell of bacon crackling in the kitchen, the loud, almost excited voices of his mother and grandmother and the brisk whisking of his father's chapped hunting pants as he came up the steps, into his room. The brass heads of the shells in his pockets grated and jingled like coins.

"Let's go get us some quail!" his father's voice boomed as he sat down on the bed.

"Mom and B-mama up?" he asked.

"They've got breakfast all cooked."

"When are we going to make syrup?"

"About midday." His father smelled of canvas, and the coolness of the outside was still on his clothes. "He's going to cut the wood and start the fire this morning."

"I want to help him," he said. "Can I go with you tomorrow?"

"Sure." His father hugged him. "I'll find out where all the coveys are so we'll be sure to get them tomorrow."

As his father rose and walked back downstairs, he almost jumped from the bed to say he would go, in a way wanting to walk behind the pointers with his BB gun (for he still had another three years ago before he could use the 410) and watch him shoot. But instead he sank back, hearing his father take the gun off the rack and the back door slap as he went out.

Still in the bed, he half-dozed, warm, under the quilts with the dusty light filtering in through the venetian blinds. Then he picked it out and sat up. He listened carefully. At first it was the regular drumming of shoeless hooves against the hard-packed clay of the avenue. They're through the gates, he thought, fully awake. Jingling, it intensified, and he could hear the creaking as the wood of the wagon rocked and swayed, frame and long boards chafing together. By the time he was at the window, his small face peering down three stories, he saw the cypress-board wagon break through the mossy overhang of the avenue and out into the open as it clopped around the house, across the yard to the shed at the edge of the pecan grove. The old man, reins cradled loosely in his hands, wore an olive-colored hat and a heavy coat, and the back of the wagon was piled high with the long, purple-green poles of cut cane.

Outside it was white cold, not snow, for there was no such thing in the South Carolina autumn, but a crystalline mat of frost spread heavily over the flat lawn, around the lined bases of the pecans and into the stubble of cut corn, all the way to the vague tree lines and hedgerows shrouded by the slow-moving ground-mists that reached into the low-hanging branches. He could already smell woodsmoke in that mist.

Turning, he saw the black man moving large pieces of wood, with a broad axe in one hand, and the mule standing, still hitched to the wagon, shifting its weight from foot to foot in light pats on the frosted ground. He did not run as he had the night before, but rather walked meekly in a mixture of caution and respect, a manner in which you might approach someone you had wanted to know for a long time, and did know in your fancies and dreams, but had never been able to acquaint yourself with in reality. As he approached, his eyes shifted from the moving man to the stationary animal.

Sam and the mule shared that quality of size which was purely solid. And even though they were old, the man's full neck and brawny arms looked as if they were made from a flexible type of steel. But all the emanation of coldness from size was melted by his face, which was the same color as the Low-country humus and held the rounded, bulblike features, tufts of white hair curling from under his hat.

When Sam saw him, he laid the log and axe on the ground and stood straight up. "You up mighty early." His smile revealed crooked teeth. "Must a been this fatwood smelling warm what brought you out in the frost."

He said nothing, coming under the shed and peeping at the fire which blazed, flames jumping and popping under the cast iron boiler. Then, "When you going to put that mule in his holster?" He looked up at the man and then at the animal, whose long tail swished on its flank.

"Oh." Sam set the wood on the oak block. "We gonna let him rest up a while before we make him work. Dugga's getting old like me and can't move so good in the morning wet air."

"Does he eat sugar cane?" he asked, the confidence coming into his eyes.

"Yeah, he'd eat that whole wagon load what's behind him if he could get at it."

They laughed together.

"Can I give him a piece?"

"Well, I imagine a chunk might get him a little more ready to working this morning." The old man laid the axe down and ambled towards the wagon, with him already out in front excitedly surveying the stacked cane. "Now, you pick out a good piece, hear."

He pointed to one on the top, and Sam took out his pocketknife and cut a twelve-inch length, then slit it down the middle, peeling the hard covering away. He cut it in half. "Why don't you suck on that piece; that there'll please Dugga fine . . . now don't you let him take your hand." He smiled up at Sam, taking the two pieces in either hand, walking around to where the animal was hitched. He had given sugar lumps and apples to horses before; so remembering, he laid the piece of cane flat in the palm of his hand, then held it up to the mule. Its head dipped slightly, and he could feel the breath from its flared nostrils, then the soft skin of the lips brush his hand. It was gone, and Dugga munched contentedly, nothing moving but the muscles in the massive head and jaw.

"He liked that good enough, didn't he?" Sam was watching, smacking on a small piece himself.

"That old mule didn't even hurt my hand." Now he sucked the sweet juice from the cane, drawing everything, leaving only a matted stick of fibers. Seeing the old man at the block with the log lined under the axe, then hearing the forged metal bite the hardwood, resonating across the moist field air, he no longer felt tense, and he drew closer. I'm going to help, he thought. So he stood to the side as Sam split the pieces of oak and pine into fourths, axe-head slicing through the grain as if it were cleaving a melon or some other soft substance. In the breaks, when Sam grabbed another length in his bearlike hand and set it on the block, he would pick up one of the split pieces and carry it next to the boiler, piling them in a neat stack.

"You gonna help me out," the old man said and started splitting the logs into smaller sections for him to carry. "Be careful a this axe now."

There was a cadence in it now, and the boy could not so much distinguish what it was comprised of, but rather feel the wholeness of a flow as the sun warmed the damp air and burnt the haze thin. Somewhere in the paced hacking, the two pieces of wood clumping down against the bare earth, and the steadiness of Sam's deep voice over it all as he told of the hours he'd spent in the woods after deer and squirrel, the times he'd plowed all day in the hot sun behind that very mule, the good crops and the bad, the summer storms and violent tornadoes; somewhere in the boy, as he moved, glancing up at the still-powerful old man over the wood, it all flowed, fusing with the blood in his veins, passing through his frame easily in wide and languid sweeps. And he stacked the logs, listening as if time were in him, too, gently slowing.

The old man's voice absorbed him completely now: "If your granddaddy was alive he could tell you what we seen one evening when we was laying by corn. Mr. James come riding up to tell me to knock off and about that time a cloud come up out of that haze and it went dark and cold. That blue cloud spread over the sky in no time. We were trying to unhitch Willy," he said, looking over at the white mule. "Ol' Willy was a big ol' work horse, Dugga's granddaddy. He was a born worker if I can say so. His feets was as big around as that stump over there." He pointed to a grayed pine stump, cut close to the ground, the size of a pie. "And he could pull a plow all day in any kind a sun. We got Willy unhooked from the plow and over to the wagon when the wind bowed them big trees so hard looked like they was going to fall over. The dust was balling up, and for a while you couldn't see for it. In all this your granddaddy got the plow in the wagon while I hitched Willy up to it. And then we took off to the sheds." He paused, taking off the heavy parka, now in overalls and a faded flannel shirt. "Now, you've seen lightning come out of a summer storm, haven't you?"

"Yes," he said, squatting in the dirt beside one of the shed's posts, looking up at the old man. "We hear it at the beach, and it strikes at the sand."

"Well," Sam said as he chopped, "this lightning we saw

that evening wasn't like that. It wasn't like anything I'd ever seen before because it wasn't white, and it didn't hit at the ground."

He looked up at the old man, eyes gleaming with both excitement and fear.

"It was red as fire way up in the sky under that cloud, shooting every which a way. About the only thing good about it was it didn't come down 'cause if it had of . . . Lord . . . it was making a racket, sounded like a popping gun, and we was riding full out. Ol' Willy was pulling that wagon so fast it about busted up on the bumps on the road and your granddaddy was right besides me, staying there, making sure I was going to come in all right, too. But we made it back here before the rain fell, and the wind only knocked over a couple a saplings, and come to think a it, that storm was good, because it cooled things off and helped the cotton to come on."

About this time, the boy heard the screen door of the big house slap, the echo bringing him back into the morning and out of the language, the gallop with Sam and Willy and his grandfather, who for one instant, under the lightning and the wind, seemed to live again. He fumbled with the wood, eyeing his mother and grandmother walking towards them with two cases of sterilized mason jars.

"Morning Mrs. Elise, morning Miss Elsie," Sam laid the axe down, taking off his hat in a rustic type of half-bow.

"Sam," his mother said brightly. "Look at all these jars we've got for you; think we'll be able to fill them all?"

"Yessum." He pointed to the wagon. "I imagine Dugga can squeeze enough out to fill them."

"Wooo." His grandmother made her eyes open wide. "I've never seen so much cane in all my life. Sam, how did you grow all that?"

"I managed, but good dirt growed it, and the frosts held off just right."

"Well," his mother said, placing the cases under the edge of the shed. "Everybody can't get enough. We've got half of Palmetto waiting for your syrup."

Sam smiled, seeing he'd let the fire die somewhat during his story, and walked over to the pile and threw an armful of logs under the pot. "I think we've got enough so we can start with the cane; my friend here," he said, pointing with his large hand, "has been helping me with the wood. He works like a man, just like his granddaddy."

The words hung in his head for a second, Sam's talk to the ladies now wrapping him in the haze of guttural sound, easy and slow, like the smoke coming up and out of the chimney. Then they went off to work.

He had watched Sam take the cold sweet potato from a

bag under the seat of the wagon, and peel it with the knife and eat it slowly, chewing every bit of each bite before slicing the next, then drinking tea from a mason jar behind it. After that, he chewed on a slab of cold venison from the same bag, and all afternoon they had worked, Sam feeding the cane into the mill while he handed it up to him: all with Dugga walking his easy circle around them, the gears rattling and squeaking, the slight clopping of the hooves on the ground, and the man's steady voice telling the stories.

He was glad that his mother and grandmother had only come out twice to check on them and that they were now taking their walk. His father was still hunting, and by the time they had boiled the juice down to the thick amber fluid, the cold dusk air was alive with the sweetness. He looked up at Sam, who was skimming the impurities from the top of the brew with a hand-fashioned strainer, an old piece of shirttail lashed to a forked branch.

Then the feeling came again as it had the night before at an instant when Sam had stopped, and there was only the hissing of the fire, its glow flicking images on his small face and the creased denim of the man's overalls. He grabbed at the legs in front of him, and Sam bent down, holding him in his strong arms. "Looks like my little man getting tired from all this good work."

. . .

His head bobbed limply down, waking him from the half-doze, the remembrance in the heat and the steamy sibilance of the locusts. Once again his eyes rested on the mill, and he thought to himself, pushing up, I don't even know what happened to them, I don't even know if Sam and that old mule are alive. For some reason he felt like hitting himself. You look at a broken machine, and you remember how you forgot about people. You go away, and you forget. Then he picked up the plate and empty jar and looked hard at them both. They still may be somewhere. On the way in, he glanced at his watch and realized there was only five minutes of lunch break left.

All of the drive back, he was hot. It came from inside, even though the wind whistled in through the windows at seventy-five miles per hour. For some reason he didn't feel like working this afternoon, even though he would only be hauling wheat, driving the large truck, which had a radio he could listen to, from field to field and then finally to the grain elevator. In the morning he had worked a fencerow with a bush hook and axe. First he had chopped the vines that choked the rust-eaten wire, then clipped it from the cedar posts, rolling it into lengths down the line. He thought he was going to return to the same work in the afternoon and pull the posts, but Mr. Powell, his boss, had told him before lunch he would drive the truck instead.

He liked the physical work involved with the fence, the sweat that broke, and it came as a relief to the solid month before that he had spent on a tractor, preparing land and fertilizing corn. But all morning he had thought about the fences, and when he realized what he was doing it began to irritate him. The fences meant something to him that he couldn't quite describe to anyone. Ten years before, when he had gotten his first gun—the single-barrel 410—he had squatted by them on the dove hunts, blending fully with the cover. The birds would always be low by the time they winged over, and at the last second, he would stand and shoot without them flaring. Years before that, almost before he could remember, the fence had held cattle and marked the pastures. But those animals had gone with his grandfather. And now the fences were finally disappearing, too.

Even though it was his farm he had worked on, worked on all morning, his fences—actually his mother's, but he would own it after her—he had done work that he inwardly opposed. It was all part of his learning about farming, so that he could run the place after he finished college and moved from the city into his grandmother's large and abandoned house.

The fact was simple; the fact came in a piece of paper

that had been signed eleven years before and was renewed each season. C. W. POWELL FARMS, INC., ran his farm now, and he was on its payroll. It had leased the six hundred acres of open land after his grandfather had died, after his family had found they couldn't run the place with old Sam, trying to break the rising costs with a hundred head of Angus, a fifty-acre cotton allotment and the remaining acreage in row crops. At first, while Sam was struggling by himself for six years, his family had started cutting the timber to help. But when a year of drought, which caused Sam to plant everything the next year in the bottom fields, was followed by a year of flood, everything was drowned out and scalded. They had gone under, and the only thing to do was to let Sam go. When all of that had happened, he was eleven; the news was distant, and the only time he went to the country then was to hunt in the winters.

Since then, with the contracts renewed each season, all was part of Mr. Powell's corporation—a larger acreage based in Barnett that grew winter rye and wheat, then corn and soybeans—3,524 acres to be exact, spread over two counties in many tracts, with an army of machinery, a fertilizer factory, a certified seed store and a chemical dealership to nourish it.

Fences divided fields that needed to lay open uninterrupted so that the tractors and combines could sweep over them swiftly. And he was beginning to feel this need, the urgency of quickness, now that he had worked for Mr. Powell for a month. The land had to be prepared, the crops planted, then inoculated with the chemicals—the fungicides, nematicides, herbicides, and pesticides—then cultivated, sidedressed, sprayed with the foliar fertilizer, and finally harvested so that the next crop could follow. With the tremendous acreage it was a continual process, the machines running in line from field to field, lease to lease, county to county, doing it from sunrise and sometimes late into the night.

He likened the whole thing to an enormous, man-made cycle constantly in motion, trying to keep up with or outdo the natural ones. One evening, when he had just started work, he and Mr. Powell had talked late at the office, and after explaining a lot of the mechanics involved in double cropping such a large acreage, Powell had said, "Once you get a jump and get things going, you gotta bust every bit of ass to keep them rolling in this business." And now, after watching the whole thing for a month, he believed it even more than he had that night, for it looked as if the farmer had never stopped a day in his life.

The big tanks of the fertilizer plant jutted up as he neared Barnett. Slowing, he bumped into the yard, with the trucks and tractors parked and scattered between the galvanized sheds and tanks. On the fringe of the grounds, in front of the woods, were the stripped frames of the old machinery, some on blocks and tangled with vines and grasses, sun-baked cultivator frames and rusted-out fertilizer trucks, a wheelless combine with the paint scorched thin, and tilted, with the cab glass shattered. Out in front, though, in the middle of this haphazard semicircle of fallen equipment, were the five red combines, new Massey Ferguson 460's, lined up as if they were airplanes, proud and ready, waiting to be catapulted from the deck of an aircraft carrier. In a way, the formation of machines reminded him of his boss's past, and the stories he'd heard about how Mr. Powell had built everything up in only fifteen years, starting at first with only two hundred and fifty acres. He was a hard worker and a good man.

By the time he parked his truck in the lot behind the office, the combines had shifted into line at the fuel pumps. As they waited, the drivers, all uniformed in gray cotton trousers and light blue filling-station shirts, three black men and two white, talked in a straggling group, half-squatting with their cigarettes and tool boxes in the scant shade cast by the machines.

There was no breeze in the yard, only a dry, set-in heat. He walked toward the combines to ask the driver what truck he was to drive, but Mr. Powell swung around the shed, the white truck rattling towards him. As it beat closer, the metal of the vehicle glinting, the tinted glass mirrored short flashes, denying any view of what was inside; three radio antennas wagged from the roof and the large tool chest that straddled the bed rumbled, tools jolting against each other with the bumps.

Mr. Powell stopped and rolled down the window in a haze of dust. "Hop in a second while them boys fuel," he said. He wore sunglasses and a vented NK fertilizer hat.

He sprinted around the idling truck and got in. Instantly the cold air that sprayed from ducts raised goose bumps on his arms. The cab seemed busy, like a mobile office, with piles of papers and charts and folders on the seat and dash. He picked up a slide rule that converted spray pressures to desired outputs as Mr. Powell wrapped his arms around the steering wheel and talked. "You know anything about moisture content in grain?"

"No," he said, placing the rule back on the dash.

"Let me show you something, then." Mr. Powell talked with only his mouth shifting, the broad, white face set in an intense, distant gaze, and only two down-sloping lines from the corners of his eyes following the angle of his glasses. "Wheat has to dry up in the field a good bit before we can get in and cut it."

He picked up a cigar box that rested between them on

the upholstered seat, opened it, and ran his fingers through a pile of shucked wheat. "This little bit here's enough to make three loaves of bread. Seeing we only get three cents out of a loaf, though, we gotta grow an ass-load of the stuff to break our costs these days." He pointed out the window. "You looking at about three hundred thousand dollars worth of combines out there."

"Jesus!" He looked at the five of them.

Then Mr. Powell leaned over and pulled a metallic black box from the glove compartment. It had a vent on the top and a digital face on the side that flickered red when he switched it on with his thumb. "This computer here tells you the moisture content of the grain. Works for wheat and rye—the small grains—we got another one for corn and soybeans." He scooped a handful from the cigar box, and as he fed it into the vent, the compact machine's digits wavered momentarily then steadied onto the number—"1.8."

"That's it," Mr. Powell said. "We cut wheat when it's dryer than 22 percent."

"That's quite a gadget." He nodded towards his boss.

Mr. Powell rested the machine on the seat, then shifted the truck into gear, grinning. "We'll get you used to this equipment around here yet. Hell, one of these days we might have you running around checking moisture. Be better than sweating on that fence like you done this morning."

"I don't mind the sweating." He cracked the door, squeezing a smile onto his face.

Mr. Powell laughed a short, loud spurt, then nodded towards a flatbed truck parked under a shed. "Take that ten-wheel over there, put the sides on it—they're behind the shop—and take it to the twin oaks field on your place," he paused. "Where the old nigger house used to be."

"Yessir." He stepped toward the flatbed, and Mr. Powell was already gone, swallowed away in the clouded dust. He climbed up into the rig, found the gears and backed around to the shop. Letting the truck idle, he put the sides on, first propping them against the steel bed, then climbing onto the already torrid platform and hoisting them into the slots. The sweat broke quickly out in the sun, and there were already oval stains pitted on his chest and back by the time he got fueled and rolling. He headed cautiously down the highway, south and to his farm, scraping through the gears, the bed of the truck rocking sideways and forward with the unhitched support chains clapping against the wooden sides.

A cast whiteness enveloped everything that flanked the road—the rolling fields, the light clay roads that blocked

them, even the forests were pale, powdered, in their green-
ness. Almost dreamlike, he drove, only the movement of
the truck moving air through his window. The black asphalt
highway was like the top of an incinerator.

At least there was shade on the county road. Grating
over the deserted railroad bed, wooden slats jostling up
then coming down hard against the metal, he dropped
back into lower gear and slowed, nearing the canopy of
outstretching limbs. There was no real reason to hurry,
anyway, since the combines had to make the seven-mile
stretch of state highway at ten miles per hour full-throttle.
He had almost an hour, and he didn't feel like rushing or
beating the truck against the bumps on the road.

Once again he passed the gates of his farm, catching a
quick glance up the avenue with the white house and
lawns at the end. The road then dipped and curved slightly
as it tunneled into a thick head of hardwoods, and on the
other side the field spread as flat and as calm as a mill-
pond at dawn. The wheat, heavy shucks and short stalks,
was blanched and splotched in places with the remnants
of light gray mildew. Swinging back onto the faint road
along its near edge, he slowed, the truck popping and
backfiring, found a nook in the side, cocked the door
open, and waited.

For a long time he looked at the oaks: the two great, live

oaks that stood in the middle of the wheat, solid, on trunks as black as they were wide and squat, the massive muscled limbs reaching out, extending their contorted grip, then twisting upwards, gnarled, knotted and knobbed, with the silvering slick-green leaves occasionally fanning in the feeble whiffs of wind, the long turfs of Spanish moss spilling downwards.

From his vantage several hundred yards off, they looked steady and rooted, as if they were growing ever so slowly, taking and making their own time, and he pictured them spreading their limbs so wide that one day they would stretch their shade all the way across the field.

Down the line and to his left he could barely see a few of the posts of the fence he had torn down earlier that day. The bramble that he had flailed from the wire was already browning under the constant sun, and he could see the coils of wire he had stripped from the fence and stood upright. He wondered if Mr. Powell would get him to dig out the posts in the morning; he wondered if he would be pulling all the fences on the farm.

The heat seemed as if it were expanding around his head, and he began to feel drowsy. He looked hard again at the oaks, and saw a low pile of crumbled bricks underneath.

"The old nigger house," he said it aloud, annoyed,

almost mocking Mr. Powell. "He wouldn't know, would he?" And he tried to visualize the shack as it had been when old Sam and his wife, Lidia, had lived there. It took him back to the first time he had ever been there, before he started spending his summers at camp in North Carolina, before the mania of growing up had caught him and he had thought of nothing but playing sports and tailing the high school girls and drinking Boone's Farm wine until it gagged him. All attention had drawn away from the farm, and he hunted only on certain winter days when the birds were flying best.

That June day he and his mother had spent the whole morning around the main grounds of the farm, working in the two-acre garden that Sam had planted for them. They had picked the vegetables—yellow summer squash and cucumbers, snap beans and ripe tomatoes. He remembered digging new potatoes on his knees, with the fresh aroma of moist earth around him, the dirt wet on his pants, under his nails and drying there.

At midday they had driven by the field, and there was the house—an island in the spread of immature cotton —shaded by the ancient oaks that rose from the flatness, curving and arching over the single-story frame dwelling as if they were protecting it. Underneath the lesser trees —the chinaberries and mimosa with their pink, feathering blooms—the raked-clean yard was the same color as the grayed wood of the house. Wide lines of rust banded the tin roof, and it seemed as if all the colors there in the mid-heat of June—the somber, blanched earth, hues of the trees and baked metals and woods—were squelched by the steady stream of light radiating from the whole hazy sky. But there was a woman in the yard, Lidia, and she stood in the full sun, stout, with a broad hoe in her hand. Her clothes, a loud, pink calico dress and a yellow bandana, hung loosely from her robust frame, wavering like pennants in the breeze. And it was this color—the human color—that seemed to defy the heat that had driven his mother and him from the vegetables and back to the city. Lidia moved with her hoe, weeding the garden, small pats of dust rising with every fluid stroke.

As they had pulled closer and stopped, she had waved. Then they had gotten out, and he had followed his mother over to the brown woman, who narrowed her eyes in the hard sun.

"It sure is hot," his mother had said, with him behind, peeping up at the aged lady still hoeing, smiling broadly, sweatless.

"Sure enough is this summertime." Lidia had stopped and leaned the tool across her broad bust and stable shoulder.

"You only raising peas and beans this year?" His mother had looked at the patch.

"Got some tomatoes around the other side," she said, nodding towards the house.

"Well," his mother had said, "Sam has surely planted us a fine garden this year. I want you to have some squash and new potatoes."

Lidia had squinted at his mother, squinted a broad, white, reflective smile onto her face and had said, "Yessum." They had all ambled to the back of the station wagon, sorting through the bushel baskets and paper sacks. Lidia had cradled her arms as his mother selected the vegetables, "Here, take some of these cucumbers, too."

Then Lidia had turned, walking with full arms to her house, his mother carrying another armload. They had gone up onto the sagging porch, then inside. He had followed, but at the last second, seeing a brood of chickens scuttling around the side, he had run around the back, the birds scattering.

A red-rusted pump stood at the edge of the shade. He had never seen one, but as he neared, something else caught his attention from the far side of the pale green field of cotton. Scuffing up a thin haze of dirt, a large white mule was walking down the rows, head bobbing with each step, a hatted black man steadying and wrestling the plow behind. Every so often they would stop, the animal stomping the dirt, then standing still, and the man would push the plow up, out of the soil, and scrape and hit the metal with something. He could hear it, resonating like a bell all the way across the heatshimmy, and as if being called by the sound, he wanted to run across the cotton and meet them. But once more they had moved, and he only eyed the wavering progression of man and animal.

Then he had pumped the well and drunk, the water spilling over his mouth and into his nostrils, making him spray most of it out in a quick sneeze. From the other side of the house, the screen door had slapped, he had heard his mother's call. Looking over at the mule once more, he had trotted past the house, the shade, to the car, where Lidia was quietly tamping tobacco into a pipe. "Thank you, Miss Elsie." She had walked back to the garden, dragging the hoe behind her. They had started the car and gone back to the city.

He raised up in the doorway of the truck, looking past the oaks all the way to the far side of the field. And where are they now? He thought hard, trying to remember exactly what had happened when Sam had left, whether they had moved far away and sharecropped on another farm or whether they'd just gone down the road, whether they had left in tears or in anger. In his mind he hunted for them, searched all the colorless shacks on the road back to Palmetto, the small farms clustered about the county. How old were they, anyway? An image of the man's gray tufts under his sweat-stained hat flashed hazily into his mind.

A breeze began to stir from the east; beyond the oaks and above the distant cypresses in the tree line, a few lines of clouds brushed, low and confused. Then from behind on the shaded road, he heard the convoy of combines, the unsynchronized dronings of the diesels intensifying until they broke around the curve, their kicked-up clouds of dust rising above the trees. They were on the field, the drivers pulling the levers from behind the glazed glass of the cabs, dropping the headers that paddled the wheat into steel maws, then clipped the stalks low, sucked them into metal gullets, shucked and separated the grain, beating the husks back onto the ground. They rolled into a staggered formation like red monsters crawling around the field, belching up a haze of black smoke and dust, so that he couldn't see them by the time they reached the far end. But the sounds permeated the air—the shearing and rattling, paddling and beating, all behind the wails of the engines as they harvested the crop.

Mr. Powell drove up next to him, and he jumped down from the cab, still eyeing the cloud on the other side of the field, beyond the oaks.

"They had any trouble yet?" Mr. Powell asked from the truck.

"Nope."

"Good enough." He grinned. "We keep them suckers running, we'll have the whole crop in in a week." Then he cocked his hat up, leaned back and said, draping his arm out the window, "You see Kojak last night? That bald-headed cop won't stop at nothing . . . will he?"

In an hour's time the field was all stubble; he and Mr. Powell had driven to the combines only twice to tighten loose belts. Now the machines lined up at his truck, spewing the wheat, one by one, into the bed. He watched from the ground, and after they had all emptied their bins, Mr. Powell called him over to his truck. "How about looking in back there and handing me that burning torch?"

He found it and gave it to his boss. "What you going to do now?"

"We burn off this stubble here so it'll decompose quick when we turn it under. Hell," he said. "I'm going to have you on that old 1155 planting beans in here at the end of the week. Got a match?"

He fumbled in his jeans, pulled out a book and lit the torch that was fueled by a small cylinder of mixed gas and diesel. "What about the woods?" He pointed. "It's dry."

Mr. Powell nodded sideways towards the edge of the field and smiled. "Came in here yesterday evening and cut some firelanes."

He rattled off down the side of the field and when he got to the far end, he dropped the torch, crossed the hedgerow, a line of fire spilling into his trail. Then the flames jumped tree high. Like a broken wave, a cruel and jagged wave, pushed by the easterly wind, they rolled and tumbled across the field, popping and clattering, sucking every bit of air towards them, throwing a column of black smoke behind. Locusts and grasshoppers clouded ahead of the fire, trying to escape, but they were caught in twisted currents of draft and pulled into the flood of flames.

He didn't even have time to think about the oaks before the heat hit him, as if a furnace door had been opened, knocking him behind the truck, the combustion ringing wildly in his ears, the smoke choking him, watering his eyes. But then it stopped at the sandy road. The gray piles of smoke filtered quietly upwards, browning the afternoon light in a shimmering pillar across the sun. Coughing and sneezing, he groped from behind the truck and saw the two great trees flaming over the parched field. Crackling, the leaves and moss were inhaled thirstily. Violent updrafts twisted the great limbs in seemingly painful spasms. He stood paralyzed, staring at the oaks, mouth agape, eyes glazed, and didn't see Mr. Powell's truck until it bumped up next to him.

"What about the oaks?" he spat out dust-caked saliva,

as Mr. Powell rolled down the window. "What about the goddamned oaks!"

For a minute, Mr. Powell said nothing, his eyes shielded by the polarized glasses. Then he put the truck in neutral. "I reckon the break around the trees didn't work."

"Look at them!" He drew tight. One of the limbs cracked and fell to the ground. The earth seemed to jolt, his muscles flexed, jumped, almost popped, and he grated his teeth hard, ready to hit Mr. Powell in the face, to catch him square in the nose and bust his dark glasses off. He held, though, trying to consume his anger, quietly.

"That wind made it burn quick, high. Usually it burns low and easy. Hell, sometimes you have to light a fire two or three times to get it across the field." He took off his glasses and there were lines pinching around his deep eye sockets. The years of ceaseless work had made their mark in his eyes. "I reckon we forget sometimes . . . about the wind, the little things."

Then he dropped his head and moved his boot across the top of the scorched ground. Looking up, he drew a deep breath and let it out. His heart jumped at his Adam's apple, the blood swishing, hot, through his head.

"Trees like that take a long time to grow," he said, and his voice faltered, glancing at them once more.

"Two hundred years," Mr. Powell said. "Listen, the

corporation will pay you and your mother for them; it's part of the lease. I've got insurance. Anyway, the field will tend easier without them."

Once again a flash of anger burst through him; his fists tightened. But he made himself go lax, and only shook his head.

"Well," Mr. Powell shifted the truck into gear. "We got a fifty-acre field to cut this evening. Follow us over to Harrison's Swamp."

He looked at his feet and only bobbed his head as Mr. Powell rattled off. Then he heard the combines break their sonorous idle, wailing, one by one, as they fell into line and left down the dirt road.

He didn't want to look back at the trees or ahead at the running machines as he wandered towards the truck. He could still hear the flames on them, picking and popping, an occasional branch crashing down.

There was a reality in them, though, a reality in their combustion and consumption and the ashes that were beginning to flake from the wood. For an instant, it almost made him feel nausea, with the heat and smoke still in his head.

But as he reached the truck on the road at the edge of the field, his sweat calmed, and as he stood in the shade of the big trees there, it cooled. The large cloud of smoke that had rolled across the field was west now, high and darkening against the sun like a thunderhead. And as he watched it wafting upwards, pulled in billowing swirls, it was as if he were rising, too. He could see the country fanning out below him—the blackened field like a small wound surrounded by the deep bottomland and then the white clay road softly winding through the pine plantations and fields and hedgerows. The land spread out as far as he could see, patient in its solitude.

"One day I'll build my fences back and burn my fires carefully and more. . . . Remember this—all of it. Learn now. The trees will grow." And gradually the shape of the rising smoke began to pull him in, reminding him of something he had never really seen before, only in his fancies and dreams. It was all before him, bigger than life, seeming to bond with him forever. And out of it he could begin to hear the voices—the stories—covering like a protective balm, strengthening him, directing his imagination and vision. He could see it all clearly—the smoke now dust, kicked-up white clay dirt, scuffed by the hooves of a work horse at full run, a big-shouldered horse and a black man and a cypress wagon with a horseman at their side all the way; all trying to make it home before a summer's storm.

FEBRUARY QUAIL—A SKETCH

The sky is that bland shade near gray, almost white. No breeze stirs, and a feeling of thickness, of cold dampness hangs, holding the woodsmoke in the tops of the trees. These are the best days, he thinks, as he widens his gait, checking the intricate movement of the dogs as they weave randomly sniffing and loping through the wiregrass. There is always the woodsmoke in this Low-country, rising from the warping clapboard shacks with their charred chimneys and soot-blasted stove vents, then misting out over the fields in a thin, gruel-like haze, curling and wrapping around the hedgerows and forest heads. And the hue of these houses that dot the countryside—the bleached colors of the cypress boards, the tin roofs that have been pelted by the regular summer showers and ooze their rust slowly, and the cold bare yards of raked clean dirt—is a soft, subtle blend. That's what this Low-country is, he thinks, watching the two pointers work around the thicket of bicolor. It's soft even when the raw air bites.

The walking has made him feel warm; his ears, though, are red and tingly and his nose drips lightly. All the while his khaki pants, chapped with heavy canvas, grate through the scattered briers, and he looks down at them every now and then and the boots that are old, oiled, water resistant. He wears a game vest that is the same rusty color as the damp grass surrounding him, and there is a muddle of noises as he moves—the distant crackling of the dogs, the twigs and leaves crunching, and in the same active cadence, the light whisking of the baggy pants and the muffled clink of the shells in his pockets. A hot breakfast of sausage and eggs, fried tomatoes, and grits is no longer in his stomach but spread throughout his body into the limbs, powering him not with explosive energy but an enduring, paced strength, one that will stay with him all day in the woods, behind these dogs.

He is working towards the far line of the farm, coming from the house through most of the fields that lie fallow with the broken stalks of corn or the close stubble of cut soybeans. Some fields are lime green with the sprigs of winter rye needling the gray soil. Here, in the late evenings, deer come to feed, leaving their cloven prints in the moist earth. He has hunted the edges of these fields where there is thick cover, and only once have the dogs birded, and only once has he shot, and missed, as the quail sailed behind a pine at the same moment he squeezed the trigger.

But now he has a whole day of burned-over sandy hills to hunt, with no deep thickets or cluttered scrub oaks, no buildings or barns to block him—nothing but the amply spaced longleaf pines and the single-acre game patches sown in lespedeza bicolor and brown-top millet.

"Hunt a bird," he shouts. "Bird in here, hunt close."

He motions the dogs back into the feed patch and only their backs and tails flag, cracking the stalks and rusty grass, exuberant in their new command.

They have energy. He looks at them bobbing and circling as they sniff the ground with palpitating noses. They are the true athletes, he thinks, and almost laughs at himself, remembering how he used to lay panting like a stuffed goat at his summer football practices from running a few forty-yard dashes. This is their life, they're professionals, and they're true to it.

The German short-hair snaps quickly to his right and stiffens, with his broad flank muscles tightening under soot-dappled skin.

"Careful, hold, Major, careful," he warns the pointer, then looks for the other dog. "Careful, Mike, hold."

The English setter is backing Major's point, and they are both crouched, easing up on the scent, the warm waft of blood that mingles with the broomgrass, luring them slowly onwards.

I wish I could smell it, he thinks, lining up behind the dogs and bringing the gun, the rib-barreled "over and under," up into a crouch like that of the dogs. He is at their flanks when they leap. The birds explode over the patch, pitching, strewn. Picking one bursting out over the edge of the plot and covering the bird with the bead, he fires, and it falls.

"Dead bird," he says and then the dogs that were frozen into the covey-rise spring towards the dishragged bird and bring it back to the hunter. Pulling the shell out of the breached gun, he stoops and pats Mike as the dog releases the quail, spitting and sneezing out the feathers, some still sticking to the pink shingles of his gums.

"Let's go get them singles," he tells the dogs, and here, out in the woods, the thinned and groomed flatwoods, he likes to hear himself talk like that: "them singles." He motions the dogs towards the area where the bulk of the quail pitched, and again the tempo of the hunt is found with the dogs weaving through the grass and the hunter behind them, reading the movements of the animals.

In these woods, he thinks, there is no time on a day like this when the sun dozes behind the thick blanket of clouds, no motion except for me and these dogs and these quail. All else is timeless in its own circular time—the slow generation of the seedlings through the tannic soil and their growth upwards, tall and solid, and then their fall and return to the humus. All is so paced and calm. Even the animals in this forest seem to fit—the deer that bed and feed by their own intrinsic patterns; the wild hogs that rake and harrow the bog holes and swamp with long snouts and sabrelike tusks; the birds of prey that sweep silent arcs in the sky, then dip into the forest, scanning the ground for any hint of a scurrying shrew; and finally the smaller animals that move by night or creep and grub around the hollow tree trunks and ditch banks.

Now, as he follows the wavering tails, the brown-splotched backs down into a slight sinkhole, they draw into a point, not tentative but definite, their muscles suppling, their tails straightening (Major's docked stub trying to), and only the eyes moving, back and forth from hunter to birds, not really seeing but visualizing through smell and knowing.

"Hold, hold on them birds, careful," the hunter says and then stops and views both dogs in their cast position, solidifying into iron shapes with a mural of gentle woods, the silvering greens and mellow browns, behind. "Yeah, hold on that birdy, Major," he says again and steps up behind them, making the vibrant cracking that startles the birds, a pair, a cock and a hen, into frenzied flight. He swings the gun slightly under, and beating their angle, fires. The first shot still echoes while the second blasts, and both birds fall.

He breaks into a run but stops, letting the dogs race ahead and do their job, receive the formal caress as their sole reward. "Dead bird," he bellows, not really having to utter this command but doing it to be consistent. The dogs double up, retrieving the folded fowl, and then they saunter back, making a pass at the hunter first, heads up, showing off the quail cradled in their mouths. Then Mike, with his matted chocolate-chip coat tangled with cockle-

burrs and beggar's lice, waggles up and drops his prize at
the hunter's boot. The dog's head tilts slightly downwards
as his master runs his hand from ears back to the shoulder
blade and then gives the setter two hearty raps on the
ribs. All this time, Major, never letting his head drop,
strutting and boasting his wide chest, prances up with his
liver nose quivering and a breast feather glued to the end
of it and pushes his quail into the squatting hunter's lap.
"Good boy." He grabs the animal's muscled neck as if
kneading it, then slaps the dog on the shoulders. "Hunt
on in here, hunt a bird!" He boosts them forward, and
they hunt.

What dogs! he thinks, watching their buoyant movement as he slips the birds into his game pouch, feeling
their warmth and downy plumage. A bird dog is a toned
combination of animal and partner, not in excess of either
quality, balanced. He has enough instinct to kindle his
nose and drive him through thicket, brier scrub, over
barbed wire, and along boggy swamp fringe after that
scent that has a natural register deep within. At the same
time, he is enough of a gentlemen to go where the hunter
wants him to, to hold a point when every muscle in him is
fidgeting, tantalizing him to bust the covey wide open. He
is enough of a partner to drop the warm bird with its
oozing blood into your hand, and accept for it a pat on the

head and an order to start again. "A dog, just a dog," he says. "But a hell of a good one."

In the rutted road that frames the dogleg of a field of harvested corn, they find a puddle. Lapping and rolling, the dogs fill themselves and stretch out, huffing small clouds of white. It's as good a place as any to break, he thinks, crossing the fence that the dogs bounded effortlessly. Finding the base of a white oak, the hunter breaches his gun, slides down and pulls an apple from his pocket, along with a penknife. He slices small wedges and puts them in his mouth, chews them around, drawing the sugary moisture from the fruit. During this time the dogs come out of their puddle, shake, and are wagging around the hunter. Finding a place, they too sit.

"Y'all want that swamp covey, don't you?" he says, slinging his arm across the nape of Major's neck. "I reckon that's where we'll head, then we'll circle it back around to the sawpile and to the house, see what we can find up that way." He knows all this talk is unnecessary, that the course around the farm's quail land is a natural circle to the animals, for they have hunted it as much as he and know the coveys. Nonetheless, spirited by the mere tone of the utterance, the dogs wag as if they already know that they will find more birds, intercept them on their convoy from roost to feed, and that more will tumble from flight.

"We still got to get them two in one shot," he says, seeing the momentary burst as the pair of quail get up; wings beating thunderously, they hang before him, then as if hurled from a catapult, they bolt. As their paths merge, the bead blots them. He squeezes at the moment of intersection, and they tumble from a cloud of feathers. With the dogs bouncing back into the wiregrass, weaving, following the faint threads of scent knit with the ground cover, he slips the last wedge of apple into his mouth and pushes up.

Their undeliberate course is pulling them down the hill to the sink of the swamp fringe, where the groomed woods dip, walled out by the massive stands of cypress and sweetgum, water oaks and a tangle of myrtle underneath. "Hunt careful down in here, careful on that birdy." He stops and watches the animals move up and down the fringe, never entering but combing the area of transition, the firelane between man's woods and real woods. Then Mike draws into a fresh scent, darting halfway up the feeble incline, then down again until he locks into it and stalks into the point. Major acknowledges.

"All right." The hunter moves down, hoping the quail will fly out into the open, for it's his only shot.

Before he's set, the birds flush in their slurred blast and are swallowed up by the deep woods with wing-beats spreading and the cocks already down and peeping, "bob-white," calling their hens, trying to regroup somewhere deep in the heart of the swamp. The many times since Daddy first brought me into these woods, he thinks, with my single-shot 410 and me not being a head and a shoulder higher than the brown grass, that I've blindly blasted at the impregnable cover of these woods with the birds safely shielded by their habitat. . . . "No," he says. "It is best to save the powder."

"Hunt in here, birdy up in here." He motions the dogs back onto the hill, eyeing the solid fortress, mapped with its brambly barbed wire. And the dogs are hunting their circle back towards the house, making their spirally movement, always in movement, in the early afternoon that shows no differently and seems no later than the quilted February morning they started out of, with the woodsmoke in the treetops and the detached sun not wanting to shine its force, only spread out in the clouds and radiate softly, softly. These woods! This Low-country! He walks in its circles and cycles and says to himself and the pointers out in front of him, "Hunt close, careful, hunt close," under the gray sky that knows no time and the land that knows no more than what's above it.